THE
SHORT STORIES
OF
RON IDDON

THE
FOURTH
COLLECTION

Published by Leopardwood Productions, P. O. Box 4818, Toowoomba East, Queensland, 4350, Australia

Iddon, Ron 1940 –

The Short Stories of Ron Iddon – The Fourth Collection

ISBN 978-0-646-98081-2

Contemporary and historical Australian life

Book design and layout by Steven Wilson – *stevenwilsondesign@gmail.com*

Type-set inTrajan Pro and Palatino, 9-22pt

Printed and bound by Lulu.com

ACKNOWLEDGEMENTS AND THANKS

To Letitia Gregory, reader of the first drafts of these stories - my 'gatekeeper'- and then to Paul McNally, Jim Durack and Jane Grieve, road-testers of subsequent drafts, and then to those numerous friends who kindly proof-read the efforts that appear here.

RON IDDON

THE STORIES

ONE

NIGHT OWLS

It is nearly midnight. His wife has taken one of her pills and will be out to it for several hours. It is a good time.

He puts the torch into one pocket of his jacket and the felt pen into another. At the back door of the house he switches off the security light before slipping outside and walking to his car under the porch.

When he is sure there is no other vehicle using his street, he backs his car out and moves off as quietly as he can. He follows the back streets until he reaches the edge of the town. Once on the highway he accelerates, heading west this time. His destination is sixty kilometres away.

When he had seen her near the supermarket earlier in the day, he had felt the familiar spasm of hatred. Now he feels calm---happy almost. He is about to do what he knows he has to do---to her and all women like her.

***

He and his wife had been living in the town only a few days when he first met Helen. He had been coming out of the hardware store;

the house the company had rented for them had needed some tap washers, and he had decided to install them himself.

She had been carrying several small rolls of wallpaper and she dropped some. He had put down his own package and helped gather up the rolls. He had had an initial impression that the woman was attractive but when he was closer and able to look her full in the face he saw that she was beautiful---short black hair, grey eyes and full, bright red lips. He was rendered almost speechless.

She said her car was parked nearby and he offered to carry the rolls to the car. After he had laid them on the back seat, she had thanked him again, and then introduced herself. He had done the same and she had put out her hand. Taking that hand in his had sealed his infatuation.

***

Though he had kept watch for her, he had not seen her again for two weeks until, as he was driving past the town's up-market motel, he saw her talking to a couple beside their car near the entrance. He stopped a short distance away and watched her go back inside the Reception area after the couple departed.

A day later he pulled up at the motel and went into Reception; he would ask if they---she---had a district map. She was there behind the counter, and remembered him. They chatted and he asked for the map, which she did have, but the meeting passed in a semi-blur for him. He had to restrain himself from staring; he thought her the most beautiful woman he had ever seen. And she was so friendly--- to *him*. He felt euphoric.

In the following week, while he worked at his job, he found he was always thinking of Helen. He took every opportunity to walk through the main shopping area, in the hope of seeing her. Only once did he do so, and then it was just a glimpse, as she was driving her car; she seemed not to see him.

He took to driving past the motel, and did see her once on the lawn. He tooted and she waved, but he supposed she was accustomed to doing that to passing drivers; he doubted that she had seen who it was.

In the middle of the following week he called at the motel office again; he said he was looking for another map. She found it, and he gave some reason for wanting it; she talked with him until some guests arrived.

He did not see her at all in the ensuing days---in the street, in shops, in any hotel---and not even when he drove past the motel, which he did now at least twice a day, very slowly.

He called at the motel office a third time, on the pretext of learning her recommendations for motels between Brisbane and their town; he said they were for some friends who were intending to drive up. She was more business-like this time, and less inclined to chat.

Lying in bed that night beside his sleeping wife, he went over the visit in his head. Had Helen been more brusque? Was she pushing him away? Or had she been simply busier than usual---had other things on her mind? He came to the conclusion that she still liked talking to him---and he had found out that she was a divorcee, and apparently had no current partner.

He thought that if he called at the office a fourth time she would probably realise that he was interested. But was it too soon to do that? He hesitated for several days.

***

"Not another map?"

"Helen, I'd collect maps every week if it meant talking to you." There, he had said it. What would she say?

"You're a devil Jim. Which map would you like this time?" She had moved swiftly past the advance.

"No, I mean it Helen. I was wondering if you would like to have a drink up at the Golf Club one evening?"

"That would be nice. Friends and I have a more or less permanent table there. I am sure they would like to meet you and your wife." Snookered. So quick, so smooth.

He had covered his disappointment, said he'd work out a date and left as soon as he could. And that night the rage began to grow in him. The bitch! She had been leading him on. Probably done that to half the men in the town. Thought she was too good for any of them. Too good for him anyhow. But who did she think she was? She was just a tart who ran a motel. He'd hired and fired women who could have run rings around her!

Within a few days he had decided he was not going to let her get away with it.

***

He passes no other vehicle this night. This is good; if someone has reported the graffiti to the police they might be on the lookout. But he doesn't know if anyone would have bothered. It certainly would have been seen, not least by the couple employed to clean the district's Rest Areas. He wonders what they thought. Probably nothing; they didn't look too bright.

But others would have read his words, particularly tourists. And some locals probably---and they could be putting two and two together. The lady should be getting some pretty funny looks soon, in town and at the Golf Club.

Would someone bother reporting them to the police? But even if they did, he didn't think that Sergeant would do anything. *There* was a hard nut; he'd probably think it was funny.

***

He slows as he approaches the Rest Area. No-one here. He pulls up in the centre of the parking area, switches off the engine, gets out and listens. Nothing; on still nights you could hear a vehicle twenty kilometres away. But if he did hear one, he'd have plenty of time to write his message and be gone in his car long before it arrived.

He takes out his pen, sits on the toilet seat and leans towards the wall.

***

As he walks back to his car he feels released. And he knows he will never feel any remorse about what he is doing, it is all her fault after all; she'd brought it on herself.

He drives back into the sleeping town. No-one will ever know---no-one will even suspect.

***

In his bedroom at the back of his parent's house he is awake, and listening to the car returning. He has heard it before. He wonders where the man went.

Were he and the man the only people in the town still awake? Was the man like him---like a possum? *There* was a possum now---no, two---in the Townsend's---in their Jacaranda he'd bet. They'd start another fight soon.

People didn't know you could hear lots of things at night. Not just possums, birds too---and cars. When he went for walks he heard lots of things. Even people talking inside their houses.

You could see things at night too---in the back streets, where there were no lights. If people wanted to come with him, he could show them a hundred possums---in the trees, up on roofs---up on the wires. They were really friendly---he could feed any of them. And there was the night he'd taken some meat to see if he could feed an owl and the bird had landed on his outstretched arm. That was a surprise, that first time. Now the bird came whenever he saw him. He hadn't told anyone that though; people didn't always believe him when he told them the things he saw. And how good his hearing was. He could even hear when Mister Harper peed in his toilet, and that was four houses away.

He could tell friends though. His parents worried he didn't have any friends, but he did. Older ones, mostly---like Mister Charters ---and Constable Damian. Mister Charters had terrific dogs---really friendly. The dogs seemed to like him as much as they liked Mister Charters. That was funny. There was the owl now---in the Silky Oak. He could get his own dinner tonight; it would be his breakfast really.

He didn't like the Sergeant but he liked Constable Damian. Sometimes he let him ride in the police car at night. He bought him an ice cream too at the garage, if it was still open. He hadn't believed him at first when he said he knew the sounds of all the cars in town but he showed him. He even knew who was *driving* each car. That was *Mister* Parker---Mrs. Parker didn't go round corners like that. Why did he drive around so late? And different directions on different nights?

He'd ask Constable Damian tomorrow about Mister Parker---he might know where he went.

TWO

AFTERNOON TEA
IN THE HIGH STREET

"Hugh....."

I turned, to face a smiling woman, of medium height, with a round, pretty face and a soft, full figure; a description I had once read came to me---'a rose of a woman'.

"Sarah Parker," she said, "how do you do; I hope I may call you Hugh? We have been so looking forward to meeting you."

I already knew that the mother of my son's intended came from the Western Districts of Victoria but even if I hadn't I would have picked it from those few words: the projection, the articulation---the traces of English upper class accent.

I took the hand she extended and then leant forward and kissed the cheek of my son's future mother-in-law, as I had, in earlier days, kissed the cheeks of dozens of women with voices like that.

***

I have spent almost all of my working life amongst cattlemen in the west of Queensland, but my childhood was in western Victoria, where my mother and all her friends had the same accent. Not coincidentally, they had other things in common: financial security, and a high degree of social confidence.

***

"Heard so much about you. Bill adores you, you know," then, before I could offer a word of reply, "oh, just the other day I mentioned your name to...." and she named someone whom she was *sure* I would know. I was able to offer only a brief affirmative before she began to list other acquaintances in her district whom she was also sure I would know.

These people, whose names I did recognise from my youth, apparently all still lived in the same region, and were all from socially prominent families. Were we about to admit a snob into our family?

I wanted to change the tack of the conversation. I had been told by my son that Sarah's youngest boy had recently returned from overseas and was trying to get a job in their area, but was finding good ones few and far between. I thought we might pick up on this ---the shortage of employment for young people---but the woman seemed less comfortable. Shortly her daughter joined us, and I wondered if she had been sent a discreet signal, as I did not doubt Sarah was capable of doing. Even my Elizabeth, reserved and unsophisticated outback Queenslander, had been able to do that.

Sarah wanted to tell me now that she had known my mother---"well everybody did, she was just marvellous". What *had* been marvellous about my mother was the genuine and kindly interest she took in people. I thought that if she were still alive she would probably have been able to tell me quite a lot about this rose.

***

Her husband seemed a straightforward man, not a particularly gregarious one I would have guessed, but acting now the role of generous host of a pre-wedding party for his daughter and my son on a winter's evening at a smart Melbourne hotel. If what Bill had told me was true, he was doing this with some grace; the Parkers' move from graziers to property developers had not gone well. They had invested in a building in the city of Geelong, and were converting it into a shopping arcade, but so far their efforts had not paid off; they were having difficulty getting the spaces rented. According to my son, the Parkers had almost run out of cash.

The wedding guest list had been kept small, this being a second wedding for both parties, but I knew that the reception was still going to be expensive. During my long drive down from my home in Central Queensland I had decided to offer to share those costs. I knew I would have to be diplomatic in how I put this, but having sized-up the husband I now thought I could be up-front.

***

The man looked at me for a second. "Well that's very generous of you Hugh, but the bride's parents always pay. That's how it's still done, I think."

"Well I don't know if it is. My daughter and her friends made all their own clothes and we had the reception at home. They cooked all the food themselves and banned all alcohol. Except champagne; I was allowed to pay for that."

Roger Parker smiled and told a similar story about the wedding of a friend's daughter.

"Well there you are. And you've already paid once for Jill. Aren't you glad we didn't call him John by the way?"

He took a moment over that and then laughed. "Yes. But really we're quite happy to pay again" (There was that "quite"; I thought

I might succeed.) He took a sip of whisky. "Actually, if you did contribute, this would be your first time."

"Exactly. So what I say is---let's make our own rules. And the rule for this wedding can be that the oldies pay for it together." The other man had nodded, and I believed we had a deal.

Before the party had broken up however the old rules had been re-established. Sarah had taken me aside and said that Roger had told her of my offer and she thanked me but really they couldn't accept. I tried to persuade her but she was surprisingly firm; I suspected I had touched on that nerve called pride.

She asked me if I had bought a gift yet, and I said I hadn't. Good, because neither had she and why didn't we go shopping the next afternoon, she knew just the place. We agreed she would pick me up in her car outside my hotel at 2 o'clock.

***

As I waited on the footpath, I tried to talk myself into enjoying the coming expedition. I do not like shopping, either on my own or in company, and on top of that I thought this company did rather give herself airs, but I reminded myself that her husband and their daughters were obviously fond of her, and Bill liked her too---and then there she was, greeting me warmly, and looking so nice.

I have always taken note of the trouble women go to in their dress and grooming---perhaps an influence from my very 'proper' mother---and this afternoon one would have had to give Sarah Parker full marks; a charcoal woollen dress, pearl necklace and earrings and a red silk scarf across her shoulders. She might have been broke but she looked a million dollars.

***

On the way to the antiques shops in the suburb of Armadale, Sarah told me she had seen the flat the couple were buying and she knew

10

what would be just right for it; two tables---a small rustic one for their kitchen and a larger polished one for the living room.

"Four hundred for each?" I hazarded. "Oh," she had laughed, "we won't get anything for that!" She couldn't say how many times she had shopped here for wedding and birthday gifts; there'd be no bargains. I was informed that we'd have to pay a thousand for each table, which surprised me a little, but as Sarah seemed to be comfortable with it, and I could afford it, I didn't argue.

***

At first I enjoyed the search, and learned quite a lot too; my companion proved to be very knowledgeable about old furniture. But though we looked at what seemed like hundreds of tables in an hour or more, she rejected one after another. "Too plain"---"too ornate"---"too big"---"too small"---"wrong legs"---"wrong shape", or "just not quite right."

Then, in one large store, when I had strayed to look at some sterling silver, I happened to glance at the security monitor on a nearby counter. It showed Sarah back in the furniture section talking to the store's manager. As the two of them walked along the aisles, I saw what I had been missing while I was by her side: anxiety.

***

We sit now at a cafe table on the wide footpath. I find myself watching her hands as she talks---touching her hair then her necklace and then her teacup---always moving. So different from my Elizabeth. Even when my wife had turned in her chair she had kept her arms and hands still; she would have pleased a portrait painter.

"You have nice hands Sarah." Surprising both of us.

She laughs and clasps them, then hides them in her lap then brings them up into view again. "Thank you, sir." But when I ask, "what are we going to do about these bloody tables?" she shrugs and momentarily looks quite helpless, and I think yes, because it's not just finding the right things, it's their *cost* isn't it, and the cost of the wedding, and all your other money worries. And if I am right you are someone who has never had money worries before in your life.

I sip my tea and, moving one of the pavement chairs aside, stretch my legs in the sun. We are out of the nippy breeze from the Bay here; I am as cosy as if I were in the sandy bed of our creek on the property back home, after I have boiled the billy and am having a short midday snooze. I close my eyes here too; I am plotting.

"We might have to raise our sights Hugh," Sarah says. I don't stir or acknowledge her words. "We might have to pay more. Why are you smiling?"

I am smiling because I recognise *spirit*. I open my eyes and watch as she pours us both a second cup.

"Why did you refuse my offer to pay for half the cost of this wedding?"

Her eyes widen. "Oh Hugh---please don't misunderstand. It was a lovely offer. We just think it's our duty to pay, that's all."

"And you thought it was just a gesture on my part?"

"Yes." Then " no!" She leans forward, earnest. "Roger and I talked about it again last night. It was really generous of you." She squeezes my arm.

"I wanted to do it for my son. And Jill. To show them I support them both." I hold her gaze, and her eyes begin to glisten. "Some people are a bit shy about second marriages. Do you know Bill originally felt that they should just have a civil ceremony---with no reception?" She shakes her head, and a tear flies away.

She looks down into her lap, at those hands now kneading her napkin. I look at them too.

12

"It was selfish of us. Of course, Hugh, we accept. Gladly. And I apologise."

"Absolutely nothing to apologise for. Thank *you*." She sniffs and casts me a quick smile. Patient recovering. I pick up my cup. "By the way, how much am I letting myself in for?" When she tells me, I pretend to almost drop the cup, and she chuckles, a rich gurgle that makes me feel quite joyful.

"Well I wish I'd known that before lashing out on expensive afternoon teas."

"Oh Hugh", and I get a tap on the wrist; she is positively beaming now.

Masterfully I push ahead with stage two of my plan. "Well, I propose that we buy just one table---between us---and that we pay no more than five hundred dollars. Total."

She nods. "Agreed."

"I don't suppose we'll get anything for that here?" But she, all confidence restored, shakes her head.

"As a matter of fact I did see something rather nice."

She takes out a small compact and begins to touch up her face. My old-world Western Districts mother held that a lady never applied makeup in public; my outdoors loving Queenslander wife had hardly ever worn any. The thought comes to me; what if the three women had met like this? Afternoon tea in the High Street. I smile at the picture. Sarah is smiling too.

"It would be perfect."

THREE

HER BIG SECRET

It's me girls, on this little thing. I found it in the bottom drawer of that desk in the back room. You gave it to me years ago Brenda; you thought I might want to put down my memoirs, which was a nice idea but I never even started. Better late than never though. "Late alright" you're both thinking.

There was a tape already in it; you probably put that in too Bren? I worked out 'record' and had a go with a few words and then hit the 'rewind' and 'play'. Working out which one was 'rewind' was tricky because the lettering seems to be almost worn off. And while I'm at it, why do they put all the controls and buttons in black--- on everything these days? I need a torch to work any of them out. I suppose they think it looks smart. I'll have to stop for a breather now.

***

Back again. And this is not going to be my 'memoirs'---memoirs--- lovely word that---French obviously; there are a lot of French words in English. You know, after William came over to England from Normandy, French became the language of the Court, and anybody who wanted to get anywhere had to learn to speak it. For hundreds of years!

Anyway---it's just this big secret I want to tell you two about, one I've kept for twenty-five years---never told anyone. *Never told anyone.* Now I'm on my way out I should at least tell you two. Someone said, "what's the point of having a secret if you can't tell anyone?" I love that. There is so much in it isn't there---our feeble strengths and monumental weaknesses. Fancy words there for an uneducated woman. Of course I believe I *am* educated---in the ways of the world, not tertiarily, if I may make up a word. And no, I'm not going to whinge about 'the hand that fate dealt me'. Have I ever whinged about that? *Talked* about it I know. In any case, I could have enrolled myself in one of those distance uni courses for the non-matriculated after my four little ducklings had flown off but, I don't know, somehow my interest in pure learning had died; life had given me too much real stuff by then. Got to catch my breath again. I might have to bring the oxygen thing in.

***

Where was I? Education, yes---but I've always been a great reader, and that educates you. I like what someone said---"if you don't read, you live one life, but if you do read you live a thousand." Good that. Back a bit I read a lot about Napoleon---just got fascinated with him. Biographies are great---if they're really well written. Thank God I got you all reading early---even Andy. You meet people in town here who don't read and you can tell. They don't know much about anything except their daily lives, and what's happening *here*. Of course television has changed that a lot---news and current affairs---but then you only get what the journalist or so-called commentators give you. It's so much better isn't it, if you're watching a program on, say, India and you already know something about the history there. But fiction educates you too. You know a lot more about people if you read novels. You have more empathy. Em-pa-thy. Don't we have such beauty in the English

16

language? Did you know there are three times as many words in the English language as there are in the French? I reckon that's why the French seem to go on and on and don't say much at all. Have you noticed that? Some French dude on television will talk on and on and our translator says the same thing in a quarter the time. It's because we are able to choose words that say exactly what we mean. I think I will bring the oxygen into the kitchen.

***

By the way, I'm sitting as I do this at the same pine table that you kids all sat around. Nothing changes. Anyhow, yes---my secret. I'm not sure what you'll think of me after this because you see---dramatic pause---your mother is a *crook*. I am. I planned and committed a crime---that makes me one, doesn't it? I didn't carry it out on my own---I had accomplices. In fact they did the work on the day. We were smart though; think of a gang robbing a bank, then think of them doing it so cleverly that no-one knows the bank was robbed. That's how smart we were. Still a crime of course. If they'd caught us we would have gone to gaol---or *could* have; we definitely would have been left with criminal records.

I hope you're intrigued? I can tell you I'm absolutely twitching ---I want to spill the beans now. And no darlings, it wasn't a bank job. "Bank job"! I sound like Ma Barker---you know, that American woman. Real baddie that one.

I'm wondering actually what this is like---for you---listening to me after I'm gone. Are you tearing up a bit? But I'm ready to go darlings. The last ten years have been hard, with this thing. Nah--- it's time. I hope for a dignified end---in my bedroom here---or, if it has to be, then in one of those back rooms at the hospital. I told you both I don't want to be kept alive on one of those machines. I doubt if we even have one here so that's good. No option.

I think this little tape recorder is wonderful. Works perfectly. 'Course now they have these digital ones. My old Webster's no help on 'digital'. I should have taken up Jeremy's offer to set his Grannie up with a computer. Could look it up there. And what about that 'You Tube'. Jeremy's always showing me things at your place on it Bren. And you can listen to concerts; I think I would have done that a lot---and used the 'word processor' too of course. Stupid name that.

He's a smart kid your Jeremy. I think you told me Bren that he's getting through uni really well. I am so glad I pushed you two through High School so that you got your Leaving. We'd have somehow found the money to help you go to university too if you'd wanted---your Aunt Ethel and me---and Reg. But you wanted to go off and be a nurse Sal and good on you; I'm sure you've been a good one. 'Course now that is a uni thing. And Brenda---you were practically engaged to that goofy Errol in school. But having the Leaving gave you options.

Carpenter Errol's a good one though---I love him. And I love your doctor Brian too Sal; you both picked good ones---better than your mother did. I don't suppose Brian's mother will turn up at the funeral. Hope not. Stuck up cow.

Sorry, I promised myself I wouldn't be bitchy about anyone; if I was confident enough I'd rewind and wipe that last bit but I'm worried I might wipe too much. I have to use a magnifying glass on these buttons! Why do they use such ridiculously small writing? I have to use a torch to read them. I must sound ancient.

Anyhow I need to get onto my big secret. Old Harrison says my clock's running down. Well I knew that! But he said months only now---maybe just weeks---and he's no drama merchant, but it could be days. It could be tonight! Harrison's always said it's emphysema but I don't know; I've seen other people with that. Remember old Phil Jenkins, he had it, but this seems different. Maybe just because it's mine.

His name's Eric you know---Harrison. It's been 'Eric' and 'Patricia' for years. I call him 'old' but he's not as old as me. I could be his oldest customer I think---or maybe Muriel Schulz; he's kept me going to eighty-five so that's not too bad, eh girls. He brought all of you into the world you know. Well, *I* did that---and could have done it by myself too. Here in the house. Easy quick births, all four of you. Not like your Eliza, Bren---twenty-four hours! Harrison's your doctor still, isn't he? Keep him---he knows all about you girls. *Girls*. Funny isn't it, you're both in your sixties but you're still 'girls' to me. I suppose Reg and Andy would have still been 'boys'. Anyhow this isn't supposed to be about doctors and babies---it's about my secret---my big secret. Be back.

***

I had a visit from the new priest in that break. Nice young man--- and don't worry I was polite; I offered him tea and cake. I suppose Eric had had a word. After he'd been here for a few minutes he dropped the religion thing; must have got the message. But he was nice---only thirty I would say. Would make someone a good husband I think. The Church's got to change there. Has to.

I've been thinking I'd like to say a bit more about education. I would really like to have been on one of those Boards that decides the curriculum because I think kids today are not being given a broad enough education. I know there are these reports coming out saying kids know more about things in the world than we did at the same age, but that's the world now---as it is *now*. They don't know much about how things *got* like this. The context. The history. How do you get any sort of a grip on race riots in the States if you don't know about the Civil Rights movement and slavery? And what sort of understanding would you have about the god-awful Middle East if you know nothing about their religions and politics? Kids today are smart, yes, but do they have *perspective*?

Jessie Corcoran has some lively kids visit her at times---her grandchildren---Lillian's. I was talking to one of them the other day when I was over there, a boy who's at uni too---I think his name is Tony. Anyhow, something came up about the Second World War and he said that he didn't know much about it---'it was before my time'. I started to tell him about what kicked it off---Germany going into Poland---but he showed no curiosity about it. It was *before his time*. They are Catholics too and all go to Mass, and I felt like reminding him that Jesus also was a bit before his time.

And that internet---what a marvellous thing, miraculous almost, and I'll bet young Tony uses it a lot, but is that *learning*? Information is only useful it seems to me when you think about it: you have to 'process' it. I agree with that person who said "data is not information, information is not knowledge, and knowledge is not wisdom." So true.

It strikes me now that I don't know when you'll be listening to this. Before the funeral? After? Together I hope, before you have to go back to Queensland, Sal. At this table would be good---sitting on these old chairs. I haven't changed anything. Still got that old dresser with the leadlight doors. Remember how you used to put all sorts of things in that little bit in the middle that was supposed to be for bread? I could never fit any bread in it. There wasn't much point anyhow, you used to go through it so fast. What will happen to the dresser? With any of my stuff? You won't need it I suppose. Vinnies might be glad of some of it. The rest can go to the dump.

I suppose you'll sell the house. You won't get much for a nineteen-fifties fibro job. Your place is lovely Bren but we wouldn't have been able to afford something like that when we got married. Lucky to get this. And it was a real struggle to pay it off---on my own. Have to pause again in a minute. 'Pause for Angelus---ding ding ding.' Remember that---on the radio? Was it 2SM?

Thinking about those early days together---I was a bit of a monster of a mother when you were young. I think I knew it at the time too. "You're the worst mother we know"; that was a good one. That was you Sal. But I had to be tough to hold us five together. I was mother and father to you and the boys. I had to be strong. We've ended up as mates though haven't we.

20

I could have had a very different life. And yes I know, you've heard this before. Humour me though loves; you won't have to put up with your mother's lectures and ramblings much longer. But all the teachers at the High School said I was very bright and determined. They wanted me to go to university---they said I could do anything---be an academic if I wanted. They said I could become a lecturer or even a professor. I think I would have done Arts---English Literature probably. Or Anthropology.

But no, the oldies decided I had to leave and get a job; "it never did me any harm" Mum used to say. I got that one in Dallimore's shoe shop. I worked with their daughter Muriel---she was one year ahead of me. It's run by her own son Ron Fink now. Still called 'Dallimore's' though. Good old family store.

Wouldn't you be prouder of me though if I was dying as a Professor---'Emeritus Professor'? You might say "but then you wouldn't have lived here Mum, you wouldn't have met Dad, you wouldn't have had us". Well---I could still have had kids, with someone else; they'd still be you, only different you. Or 'yous' as I hear some kids saying now in this town. Be glad girls that I insisted you speak properly.

***

I've decided I need to say something now about your father---about our lives together. And take that 'here we go again ' look off your faces. Can there be anything I haven't already said to you on that particular subject, you're thinking? Possibly not, but I'm wondering what impression your own kids have of Ray? What have you told them? That's your business I know, but they never met him, and by the time they met me I was on my own. So I'm going to ask a favour. All this about my big secret is just for you two---I don't know what your own kids would think about it---but I want this next bit to be heard by them. This is 'family history'. It's important. You'll have heard it all before so you might want to 'fast forward' this bit. I know there is a button on here for that but if you can work out which one it is good luck to you. Careful you don't wipe anything though.

***

Hello kids---your Gran here. I'm on my way out now but I just feel I should tell you something about my life. Particularly about your grandfather. It's important.

You never got to know him, and in a funny way I hardly knew him either---looking back. Here we go. I met Ray in this town when I was seventeen and he was twenty, and we got married when I was only nineteen. Too young I know but that was my choice. I was in love, or I thought I was, and yes even at nineteen I could see things in him that worried me, like the beer; that's all men used to drink back then. And he was hopeless with money. He'd have ten pounds in his pocket on a Friday night and next to nothing by Sunday; that was twenty dollars, which won't seem much to you but back then that was a working man's weekly wage; it would be hundreds of dollars today. I thought I could change him. Girls always think they can change boys.

Ray always had work in the early years of our marriage, when we had your uncle Reg and then the two girls, but I couldn't change the money thing. He had a job at a sawmill here, and then later at the Railways; the Railways were important in our town then--- employed a lot of men---not like now. Ray got paid on a Thursday but I really needed to be in that Pay Office so they could pay *me*, because sometimes when he'd get home late after being at the pub on pay day he'd have no money at all; he'd have lost it on cards in a back room, or two-up. (You might need your oldies to explain that particular recreational activity.)

It got that way that if he was late getting home on a Thursday I would have to go down to his pub. I'd take Reg and send him in to find his father; women didn't go into hotels in those days--- respectable women---certainly not amongst the men. Little Reg

---and he might have been only four or five---he'd give Ray the message that I was outside and that he had to give him his wages, what was left. I'd say to Reg---this *little* kid---"don't come out without it." It was humiliating but I had to do it. I wasn't the only woman who had to do that, most of them sitting out in their cars. We didn't have a car.

Ray just never accepted the responsibility of being a husband and a father. It was like it meant nothing to him. Just after I had your uncle Andy, Ray started to go away, just head out of town; I never knew where he went or how to find him. He'd come back, but it could be months later. He'd say he'd been over on the coast or somewhere---how would I know? He said he'd been working but I never saw any money. I have to take a break right now; I'm practically living on oxygen these days. Pathetic.

***

Righto, I'm back---and I'm going to use some strong words now. I'm afraid I got to despise your grandfather---actually, to hate him. Because of him I had a very hard time rearing your mothers, and your uncles. It made me a bitter and unpleasant person, not now I hope, but then. Ask Brenda and Sal. Ray eventually died of prostate cancer---and very young---only forty-three. He was buried in the town cemetery here. Your mother and your auntie went to his funeral but I didn't go. They thought that was very hard of me but I couldn't; it would have been hypocritical of me.

Well. That's probably enough said now. Except goodbye---it's been a joy to know you.

***

Back to you now girls. I'll bet you get a few questions now from your near and dear. Did you listen to it too? Do you think what I said was too harsh? I know you don't like me going on about him. You went to his funeral and I didn't, and you said but he's still our father Mum and we loved him. I remember thinking---you didn't love *him*---you couldn't; he gave you nothing to love. You loved the *idea* of your father. What do you reckon? If I wanted to be really nasty I'd say what did he ever give any of his kids but cancer? The prostate thing that killed him took Reg and Andy as well. And Andy was only thirty-nine. But that, I give you, does sound hard.

There's that great description of a drover's bitch---'all tits and teeth'. Have you ever been to a drover's camp? There's nearly always a dog like that around---and you've generally got to watch out for her. I must have seemed a bit like that to you and other people back then. I used to get pretty snarly.

***

Here again---but that was a real long break---a week. Not a good week either. Tell you the truth, there was one time when I wasn't sure I'd get back. I'm feeling okay again now but I'd better get a move on---the clock's ticking. Have to get onto this secret.

Oh---do you remember the McCorquadales? June asked me over this morning. Her two girls are up from the Murray and they asked after me.

Some mothers are like sisters with their daughters aren't they. Those three carry on as if there is no age difference at all. It's lovely to see. We three get along too but there is an age gap isn't there. But my experience of life has been so different to yours. It's as if you two have lived your adult lives in a different world. But we've had some good times haven't we---together---when you've come back here Sal. Sitting around this table with a wine. And a beer. I still like a beer. There's a generation gap right there.

I was never like June McCorquadale. She's outgoing and kind; she always gave me the impression she loved being in the company of her children. By the time you were five or six I wished I were anywhere else---I wished I were any-*one* else. In your memories of

24

your mother, was I ever kind and gentle and loving---in those days? I can't think so.

It was just the money worries all the time my dears. Like the embarrassment of having to put things on the tick at the Turtons. And I used to go to school with Sally Turton. She was Sally Bushell then. I could hardly ever afford to buy either of you a nice little dress, or decent shoes. Let alone things for myself. If it hadn't been for the money your aunt Ethel sent over, bless her---and the bits that Reg was earning after school and on weekends---I swear I don't know what would have become of us. You know, Reg used to give all that money to me. He could see how things were. Your grandparents never lifted a finger---any of them.

I've never told you this---another thing I've kept to myself---but I was that close to going to the Church and asking them to take you all for a bit. Till things looked up. It wasn't just the money---I was run down too. Harrison was worried; he'd give me that look and say "you need rest Patricia", but when could I get that? There's all sorts of help now, for single mothers and the like---and that's what I was, virtually. Your father---aah, I won't go there again; I know you hate it.

"You're the worst mother we know." That was you Sal, when you were going off to school one morning. Funny---always you girls. I don't remember Reg or Andy ever getting that stirred up. Was I harder on you two? Don't think so---didn't mean to be. But boys don't push your buttons the way girls do sometimes.

You were about eleven Sal, that time. You and Bren were at this back door, going off to school. After you two went off I sat at this kitchen table and---here's another little secret---I had a bit of a cry. You never saw me cry did you? It would have shocked you if you had come back in for something and seen that. Hold the presses again.

***

25

Okay---now---my big secret. Finally, you're saying. Twenty-five years ago this happened, but I remember every detail as if it were yesterday. Actually my memory generally is fantastic---long and short term; no 'oldtimers' here. That reminds me of something Napoleon is supposed to have said; "they have learned nothing and forgotten nothing." He was talking about the Hapsburgs---or it could have been the Bourbons. If I'd taken Jeremy up on his offer of a computer I could check it up on the internet.

But it's lovely isn't it. Haven't we all met people like that. Ooh---darlings----a pain.....

FOUR

MUM'S SECRET REVEALED

Brenda here kids. I thought I'd use this same recorder Gran did for that stuff about your grandfather. Funny that it's finally being used like this; it was me gave it to her years ago.

When she was having that heart attack she managed to ring me and I called the ambulance; we arrived at the same time. Just as well they kept her in our little hospital afterwards because she had that second attack a few days later. Sal was here before that though and we had some time with her. Actually it was a good time---lots of laughs. She picked up a lot---we thought she was going to come good. Well, we knew the emphysema wouldn't disappear, but she'd somehow managed that for so long we thought she had it under control. But then she had the stroke and that was that.

But before that, as I said, we talked a lot, about the times we had together---when we were kids. She told us we should listen to that tape and on it she went on about some crime she had commited years before. She wanted to tell us about it but didn't want us to tell you.

We heard it all but Sal and I decided you should know about it too because it is family history. Sal and I have to set the record straight. Family history makes us what we are, doesn't it.

I got the job because Sal had to go back to Queensland.

***

Mum liked to put herself out as this unsentimental toughie but Sal and I realised---when we got older---that she'd been a terrific mother. If Reg and Andy were still alive they'd agree.

You'd remember your uncle Reg of course but you might not have seen much of Andy; he hardly ever came back here. You did spend some time with him when we took that trip to Aunt Ethel's, but you were very little then.

Mum said to us girls once that she probably shouldn't have had Andy. Not that she didn't love him; the story I can tell you now shows I think how much she did. No, it was mainly the money thing---with Dad being the way he was; a fourth kid must have made everything that much harder.

The other thing that made it harder was that Andy was a slow learner. Nowhere near as quick as Reg---or me and Sal, come to that. I wonder if some babies don't get all they should, in the womb. If the mother's stressed, like Mum would have been.

Andy didn't start talking until he was three; I remember he was still wearing nappies then too. And he had a lot of trouble later with schooling; Mum was always having to go there to talk to teachers. She only kept him at high school because it was the law, and she took him out as soon as it was legal; I think that was fourteen---or fifteen.

The only work he could get at first was on the farms around here. The farmers never trusted him with their machinery apparently, but they said he was very good with livestock. Then when he was about seventeen he got a job with the Council here---a pretty ordinary sort of one, on the roads, but at least he was earning his keep. And of course he had Reg's horses to play with.

***

Reg was so different to Andy. He was smart, and always on the go. I remember when he came home from school, he'd change his clothes and go straight out again, delivering things for shops on his bike, or just working on something in our yard; he never just 'played', like us girls, or Andy.

He used to do work on farms, on weekends, and I think from the time he started high school. Mister McLeish had one of the biggest places around here---his family still does---and old McLeish reckoned that he only needed to show Reg a thing once for him to get it. He even used to let him operate his big harvester. At fourteen!

Reg did really well at school too but it was like he didn't have much use for it when he could see opportunities for himself outside school---to make money. Mum tried to get him to stay. "At least get your Leaving", she used to say---something she made us do later on---but I think he wore her down. He had all this energy and drive.

He worked after school at Gregson's garage and that man offered him good money to come and work full time---good money for those days. So that's where he went; he wouldn't have been sixteen.

What Mum hadn't known was that on one of the farms---the Svenson's---Reg used to exercise the trotters; Mister Svenson used to breed them, and race a couple, more or less as a hobby. Tom Svenson told Mum one day that Reg had a real talent for driving; that's what you call it, 'driving'.

Well, even though Reg now had this new full time job at Gregson's, he started exercising the trotters at old Col Smith's stable here in town as well. Then he started driving them in races too, and winning. Mum and sometimes me used to go to the trots when he was racing; Sal had gone off to do her nursing by then.

When he was still only twenty-two, Reg did a deal somehow with Mister Gregson to buy him out of the garage, and then he bought out old Smithie too; how he managed to get the money together for all that we didn't know, but that was Reg. Of course the Smithie deal wouldn't have cost him much; I don't know who else would have taken it on.

Next---and I know this was a worry to Mum---he decided he would work the horses full-time himself, and get one of his employees to manage the service station. Mum tried to talk him out of this; I think she thought harness racing was a pretty risky proposition, not really a business at all.

Thing is though, Reg *ran it* like a business---charging his monthly training fees up front for instance. He'd take any young horse a breeder brought along, but if it didn't perform pretty quick, he'd send it back. Ruthless really, but it meant he only ever had good horses in his stable, so his winning record was good, and this got him even more clients. Sal has a newspaper clipping from when he died that said Reg was the most successful harness trainer in Australia, outside the capital cities.

***

As I said, Andy had that job with the Council but he started to spend all his time after work and on the weekends at Reg's stables, grooming and exercising the horses; Reg even let him drive in some races. Andy really liked the animals, and had a sort of understanding with them. Reg said Andy could tell before he did when a horse was coming down with something.

***

When he was about twenty Andy moved away, over to the town where Aunt Ethel lived, and then we learned he was training trotters too. There was an old trainer there who wanted to retire, and he was happy for Andy to take over his place as long as Andy trained a couple of *his* horses free of charge; Andy must have been talked to the man at one of the race meetings.

Mum told me she didn't see how he would do any good. That town was pretty small, and harness racing wasn't real big there---nowhere near as strong as here. But on top of that, she couldn't see Andy being able to run a business; he wouldn't be smart like Reg. And he wasn't *lucky*. Mum said Napoleon---she was a full bottle on that man---she said he always asked for generals that were lucky; he certainly wouldn't have taken Andy.

Andy was living with Aunt Ethel, so that would have been saving him some money---and she was keeping his books, which we thought was another good thing. Andy never let on to Mum how he was doing, but Ethel used to keep us in the loop. She said he didn't seem to have any really good horses, and hardly ever won anything, but at least his feed bills were being covered by the training fees; he was the only trainer in her town so the breeders didn't have anyone else to go to. Ethel said Andy didn't charge much, but even so, some of the farmers were slow at paying up. Reg would have sorted them out.

Mum went out there once to see her sister and Andy---he would have been about twenty-three then. She told me when she came back that Andy's stable set-up was depressing---so different to Reg's. Reg always had his place spic and span; it even used to look good from the road---fancy gate and nice fence and trees and lawn, and a bitumen driveway. And he kept all his stables painted, and the yards too. His floats were always spotless, and at the tracks the horses wore red satin rugs.

Andy's place apparently was a mess. A dirt track in---dusty when she saw it, and probably a quagmire after rain---unpainted stables and yards---fences leaning over at all angles. You can just see it. And Mum said Andy himself was untidy too: unshaven, hair not combed. If Reg looked like a winner, Andy must have looked the exact opposite.

I don't know how it was but Mum had a bit of money put aside by then and she gave it to him to fix the fences and the driveway and paint the stables, but she did wonder if it would make any difference.

***

Is this interesting to you? I'm going on a lot about horses because they were the boys' lives really---right to the end. And this 'crime' thing of Mum's was about horses---some horses the boys had, and a big race in Andy's town.

***

Reg would have been in his late thirties, Andy early thirties, and Reg had this good mare, Gypsy Swing, one he actually owned; she won I think twelve races. Not a big animal, about the size of that Hondo Grattan who won the Inter Dominion. Similar colour too, a nice rich bay with a black mane and tail---no white on her at all. She was a real favourite of Mum's; Reg used to call her "that mare of yours." She used to put a little bet on whenever the mare was running.

Reg kept her after she finished racing and bred from her. She dropped a couple of useful foals---not as good as her, but they paid their way. Then Reg took her to this stallion that had raced against her and one that he'd always liked. The funny thing was that he looked just like the mare, same colour and height. And Gypsy King, when he came along, looked identical to both of them.

He turned out to be fast, and even better than that, a *competitor*. Reg told us that even during the training trials, he picked up his pace when one of the others came up on him. Reg was excited. Mum and I were too---a foal from 'our' mare, and looking like a winner. Reg booked the mare back to the same stallion of course.

Mum and I went along to watch King in his first race, which he won easily. That horse went on to win sixteen races in a row; the only time he lost after that was when he was given such a big handicap he got boxed in. Any race that was fair dinkum though he won.

When King's brother Prince was born he was the spitting image of his older brother, and of course we all hoped we might have another champion. Reg put the mother back to the same stallion again but she did not get in foal and in fact never had another foal. So Gypsy King and Gypsy Prince it was.

Well, Prince turned out to be just average. He would start off in each race well enough---he often led the field out---but he had only the one speed. I know the couple of times I saw him race he was still in front at the beginning of the last lap, but when another horse came up beside him he didn't fight him off. The only important part of a race is that winning post, and Reg just couldn't get Prince there first.

Reg campaigned Prince for two years then he decided he had to go; I think he probably only kept him that long because of King and Swing---and maybe because of Mum and me. Reg only kept good horses; everyone knew that when Reg turned up at a meeting he was there to win.

One night Reg rang and asked me to come around here to Mum's to talk about Prince. He was going to try to sell him, but he said he wouldn't get much for him; he might be the full brother to a champion but that wouldn't count for anything now. Reg thought he would probably end up at a knackery. Dog meat.

Andy was still not doing any better and Mum suggested Reg should give him the horse. For one thing, she didn't like the thought of the horse becoming dog meat, but also she reckoned there was a chance that, in Andy's district further west, where the competition was a lot weaker, Prince might win a race or two for him. Reg agreed.

***

Prince did win two races in the next year with Andy, but apparently they were very minor ones with next to nothing in prize-money.

Ethel told Mum that throughout all that year Andy won only four races---with all his horses.

Mum went over to see Ethel and Andy at the end of that year and when she came back she said his stables looked even more run-down than before---potholes in his driveway again and the front gate hanging by one hinge and things that needed fixing not being fixed. But the worst thing was she learned that Andy had prostate cancer, and his doctor had said it was well advanced. Only thirty five! He had never had anything checked. Men didn't then---still bad at it; don't you be so stupid Jeremy.

Mum tried to talk Andy into coming back here, where at least he'd have Reg and her and me to keep an eye on him---when things got bad---but no, he wanted to stay where he was.

He also let on to Mum that his big regret was that he hadn't won their annual Cup, the next one coming up in three months time. The "Federation" they called it, the biggest race they had there in that district. It still is, and it's always been won by an outsider. The prize-money was surprisingly high---$10,000; I think it's $20,000 now; they make a big deal of the "Federation" there.

At that time the race was limited to twelve horses, but those horses had to have won good races beforehand to qualify. Andy had no horse that would get in under that ruling but under another one he did; any trainer who actually lived in the town automatically had a right to enter. Andy was the only one at that time, and of course he was going to nominate Gypsy Prince.

Mum thought the race would probably interest Reg too; two hundred kilometres isn't that far for a trainer to take a horse if he thinks it has a fair chance of winning that sort of money. Sure enough, when she got back here she found out that he was going to enter King. So there went any hope for Prince; Andy wasn't going to win that Cup before he died. But this is where Mum's 'crime' comes in. ("at last", you're probably saying.)

"I thought", Mum said to Sal and me, "what if King won---*as Prince!*
Who would know that it was actually King that Andy was driving?
They were identical in every way."

Now, whatever faults your grandmother may have had, she'd
always been a stickler for honesty, something she'd impressed on us
on many occasions when we were little---physically at times, let me
tell you. So this was a shocking thing for Sal and me to hear---and
---what was more worrying---we *knew* that Andy had won the cup
that year; it was on Mum's mantelpiece.

Apparently what she said to Reg went like this. "You have a brother
whom we all love---he wasn't born with the abilities you have---he's
dying---this is something we can do for him, and what harm would
it really do anyone?" Reg had to cop all this while he was standing
in the yard at the front of his stables.

According to Mum he just kept looking down at the ground, as if he
couldn't believe what he was hearing. She said he just kept saying
"Mum, Mum......," and shaking his head.

Mum said he walked back into one of the stables without even
saying goodbye, and she thought that was probably the end of her
evil plan.

"Well no wonder," I said. "He'd have been rubbed out for life by the
racing people if they'd caught him. How *could* you!"

Mum spread her hands across the covers. "Well---he didn't enter
King in the race---and you know the result. You've seen the cup.
Prince's name is on it."

But had it been Prince? I can tell you, your aunt and I were lost for
words. Had Mum really talked our brothers into this? Had they
really gone ahead and swapped the horses?

I remember what a stir the result caused at the time---Prince beating
what people knew were far better horses. At a hundred and fifty to
one!

Andy I think would have been up for the con; what did he have to lose? And the swap would have been easy enough to manage I think, say at some roadside rest area late at night. And they could have swapped the horses back again the night after the race.

If the boys had done this, had Mum been kept in the loop? Because if she had been, that would have incriminated her too wouldn't it? What do they say---'an accessory after the fact'?

You can imagine Sal and I had a million questions---but we never got the answers. Mum had been holding my hand just then, and she squeezed it, made a little sound and went quiet; she was having that stroke. She didn't come round, and died a day later.

***

Well, Sal and I don't think it happened. For one thing, we had never heard anything in all those years---not a hint---not from Mum or Andy or Reg. Of the three of them we'd have most likely got it from Andy, but then he lived only another eighteen months.

And while Reg was a tough competitor on the track, he was always known as being very straight. Just a whisper of anything like that could have brought his whole business down.

In any case, horses are identified by their brands. Fire brands early on, then that freeze branding---those little numbers and symbols they put on the neck. You generally don't see them because they're up under the mane. They're very detailed, and the stewards at the tracks always check every horse.

Could they be changed in any way, I wondered---or smudged or blurred or something? I've talked to racing people about that and they say no, it would be too obvious.

So no, your Aunt and I believe that Andy did actually win the race that day. There might have been better horses in the field that day, but sometimes they can get boxed in. In himself, Prince was pretty fast; it's just that he wasn't a competitor when he was challenged.

But if he was still in the lead when they came into the last lap, and if none of the 'good' horses had been able to get out he might have been able to stay there---*must* have been able.

But your grannie believed, until the moment she died, that the boys had followed her plan. I just hope she got a few bob on, at that 150 to 1.

FIVE

MAGNIFIQUE

You think you know someone.......

***

Jane and I have been married for eleven years. If I had to describe
the woman's nature I would say it is calm---unlike mine, which
is 'volatile', she has informed me. This she did in the same quiet,
polite way she says everything. Mind you, she is no doormat; if she
has an issue with me I am left in no doubt about what she thinks,
but she is never over-assertive and of course never offensive.

***

We are both primary school teachers in a country town, but right
now she and I and our two young daughters are on holidays,
staying with her sister in the big smoke; yesterday that kind woman
had offered to look after our girls while we two had a day on our
own.

In perfect weather, we took a ride on a ferry, had a nice lunch,
walked through the old Botanic Gardens and visited the City Art

Gallery, where we knew there was an exhibition from France. By four we thought we should be heading home again.

There was a taxi rank at the front of the Gallery. There was one other couple waiting and we got chatting about some of the works we had just seen. Henri and Claire were themselves French; they managed well in English with us, but they also allowed themselves to be subjected to some of my schoolboy French. They said that they too were heading to the railway station, and I suggested we save time and money by taking the next taxi as one party.

Within a few minutes a taxi did appear and I told the driver where we wanted to go. The French pair and Jane got into the back seat and I sat beside the driver. We hadn't gone far before the woman took some tourist brochures from her bag and began showing them to her husband. They were speaking of course in French, and I know enough of the language to understand that they were discussing what they might visit the next day.

I noticed that our driver was casting quick glances into his rear vision mirror, and I detected a growing restlessness in him.

Suddenly, "speak English in my taxi! You're in Australia now."

There was a shocked silence for a moment. Then the woman said "I'm sorry---we weren't talking about you. We were just looking at these...." but the driver interrupted.

"I don't care what you were talking about, you speak English in my taxi."

The man began "but it is nothing. We do understand your language ...." *when Jane cut across him.*

"You are being very rude, driver." Her words were delivered with an authority and firmness I had rarely heard.

"No I'm not! They come here and think they can talk any way they like. This is our country and we speak English!"

"But.....," Jane gathered her thoughts. "If you and your wife were in a taxi in Paris no-one would expect you to speak in French to her. That would be unreasonable."

"Well I'm in Australia. So are they. And so are you!" He glanced across at me. "What do you reckon?" Sensible Aussie men together.

"You are way out of line here mate. Just imagine you went to China or Russia or Iceland---could you speak in all those languages?"

"You wouldn't find me in any of those places! Struth", and he veered over to the side of the busy city street and stopped. "I'm not having this. You can all get out."

The Frenchman made to open his door but Jane stopped him with a peremptory "no!" I was amazed; was this my *wife*---my gentle companion of twelve years? This stranger leant forward till her face was at my shoulder, and almost level with the driver's.

"We will not get out. You will take us to the station."

"I won't!" He turned the engine off. "We're not going anywhere. It's my cab and I decide who rides in it---and I'm not having people like that. Or you. What makes you think you can talk to me like that?"

"What makes *you* think *you* can talk to our visitors like that?" I said, and was about to say more---I was disgusted and angry---when I felt Jane's hand squeeze my shoulder; leave this to me.

"I can talk any bloody way I like in my cab! If you don't get out now---all of you---I'm calling base. They'll call the cops."

I turned in the seat to look at the visitors. They looked at me and shook their heads; let it go. Once again the man's hand went to the door handle.

"No!" Jane ejaculated, and actually reached across and pulled Henri's arm away."We are staying here---and I can see two policemen on the other side of the street. I will go over and get them," and she turned away as if she were about to open her door.

I was shocked by the driver's stupidity and rudeness, but even more shocked and, I have to admit, delighted by Jane's attack. You have to understand that this is the most reasonable of creatures---strong minded perhaps, but diplomatic to a fault. This aggression was something I had never seen. I turned right around and grinned at her; Jane told me later I actually said "go for it love."

Jane's threat about the police worked. The driver started the car and we drove towards the railway station. We travelled in silence for a while, the vehicle seeming still to be reverberating with the words that had just been said. However Jane---relentless---had not finished.

"When we get to the station, driver"---leaning forward again and looking at his identification card on the dashboard---"Rex---I expect you to apologise to Claire and Henri."

You've gone a bit too far there love, I thought, that won't happen. Rex said nothing.

When we pulled up at the station rank I paid the man. The Frenchman went to open his door but again Jane restrained him. He and his wife looked anxious; they---and I---were under the control of a woman possessed.

"Rex?"

The man looked straight ahead; he was not apologising to anyone. I too looked straight ahead; I don't know where the French two were looking. It was a tense moment.

"Rex, I have all your details off that card. I am going to sit here and call the company on my mobile if you do not apologise." Really, really firmly.

I felt rather than saw Rex's shoulders sag. "Alright. I...."

But he was stopped by "not here. We'll all get out. You too. And you'll shake hands with them."

Unbelievable---but I felt the seat move, and then the driver opened his door. We all got out, and the driver did apologise to the couple and shook their hands---not meeting anybody's eyes---then got back in and sped off.

***

Claire and Henri were going to a different platform so we said goodbye on the general concourse; they hugged both of us. Before they left, Henri looked into my eyes.

"Magnifique!" And I have to agree.

SIX

THE MAYOR

We have a good local newspaper in this part of the north of Victoria, and recently the editor asked this retired journalist if he would do a series of feature interviews with notable people in our region."At your own pace; I know you won't want to do it full time."

The commission had proved a boon to me; I had recently lost my wife, and the travel and the meetings had helped me deal with those feelings of loss and loneliness; I think this may well have been part of my friend's intent.

This particular afternoon I was amongst irrigated dairy farms near the Murray River, and my 'victim' was to be a mayor. Though the woman belonged to no political party, she had been re-elected mayor of her shire five times, and with an increased majority each time; anyone I talked to about her had only praise for her handling of the job. She was believed to be quite wealthy, and it was known that she had given substantial financial help to young people in her region, particularly those from disadvantaged backgrounds.

She had readily agreed to my request for the interview, and suggested her office in the Shire Chambers.

I was greeted by a tall, broad-shouldered and handsome woman, perhaps fifty-five years old, possessed of a direct gaze and, I soon found, a calm and confident manner.

As an interviewee Patricia Kormann proved to be a journalist's dream; everything she told me about running a Shire Council was interesting and fresh---not at all bureaucratic or dry. And her mind was so organised that it all flowed; I thought I would need to do very little 'cut and paste'.

Towards the end of my allotted time, a delegation of farmers from along the river arrived to talk to her about what they claimed was an urgent need to repair a bridge in their area. She excused herself, but then asked me if I needed to leave town straight away, and when I said no, had suggested we have a drink in the lounge of the hotel across the road from her office; she thought she would be only fifteen minutes or so.

***

In that lounge she began to tell me about some of the people she knew and worked with in the region; she did this with humour but, I thought, with kindness.

After I had been favoured with a long thoughtful look, she asked if I had the time to listen to a story. By the way she settled herself into her chair I guessed that the story could be a long one, and I ordered another round of drinks.

***

A couple who owned a farm about twenty kilometres out of a small town in this part of Victoria had married late-ish in life. Their one child, a daughter, was four years old when the mother suffered an ectopic pregnancy which was not diagnosed early enough, and she

46

died. The father had no immediate family members who could rear his daughter and he took on the job by himself.

That little girl became her father's workmate. Even before she reached school age she was bringing the cows up to the dairy. There, as soon as one cow had been milked, she would fetch another in. The man's herd was not large, just fifty milkers, but the shed was of the old walk-through type, where each cow had to be handled individually, and so the milking took more than two hours, but the little girl helped till the very end each time.

The child was given almost no opportunities to play with other children of her own age; because her parents had married late, the children of their contemporaries were a lot older. In fact, practically the only people she did meet from one week to the next were members of the father's church in town.

***

When she was old enough to go to school, she caught a bus each morning at the T- intersection at the end of their road, about a kilometre away. Halfway to the bus stop she would pass the entrance to another farm, the Pattinson's. Their boy, Nigel, three years older than the girl, also caught the bus, and they would meet there and walk the rest of the way to the end of the road together. If he were early and could see her coming, he would wait for her.

They didn't talk much, but were comfortable with each other. If either did speak, it was generally about something that had happened on their respective farms---a new calf, or a broken trough or a gate having being pushed open by the cows.

When the bus came they didn't sit together, the boy joining other boys of his own age at the back. She would sit on her own; no other girls as young as she were catching that bus in those years.

At the school in town she would go straight to her own little locker outside her classroom and put her food in there, plus any extra books she had brought. Then she would look around for her teacher, Mrs Huthwaite, and go to her. The woman had realised that the child was unused to the company of other children, and found little things for her to do until the bell rang for class.

In the afternoons the child caught the bus again and walked back part of the way with Nigel. When she arrived home she changed and went straight to join her father at the milking shed.

***

On weekends the girl helped not only with the milking but with any other chores that she could manage, like feeding the hens and collecting their eggs. In the house she swept floors and made beds. She learned to set the table, and to clear away after meals; while her father washed up she put the dishes away.

***

By the time she was eight she was able to put the milking cups on the cows, and to operate the long wooden pole which opened the exit door at the head of each bail. A little older and she was able to carry the buckets of skim milk to the pig pens.

As the years went by and as she grew, the girl did more and more of the chores. By the time she reached high school age she was strong enough and skilled enough to do any job that her father could. This was just as well, as the man seemed not to have the energy he had once had; he was losing weight, and often needed to rest during the afternoon.

The girl never resented her work-load, because she could see her father needed her more and more. What she did find hard to accept was that she was never able to go away anywhere---even on school excursions. She was not allowed to play team sports, in district competitions. "What if you were late back for the milking?" The man could have paid someone to help on those afternoons---sons of neighbours were always looking for opportunities to earn extra cash ---but he told the girl he couldn't afford it. He never took her to school concerts, or play nights, not even at Christmas. "I'm too tired. And you need your sleep too."

The girl's life was restricted to school and home---and home meant work.

***

When she began to attend high school, at a bigger town fifty kilometres further along the river, she needed to catch an earlier bus, but her father simply brought the morning milking forward an hour. By the time she arrived home again, he would already have begun the afternoon milking but she would change quickly and join him. After milking she would do all the washing down and the feeding of the calves and the pigs; in winter it was always well after dark by the time she returned to the house---where she now had to do all of the preparation for the evening meal.

The man was suddenly looking older. When, in her thirteenth year, the girl met her friend Nigel's grandfather at the Pattinson's house one weekend, she realised that he looked younger than her own father.

She persuaded her father to see a doctor, and that man referred him to a specialist, who did tests. He found he had a condition akin to muscular dystrophy; the prognosis was for on-going deterioration and probably an early death. As the condition was somewhat heritable the father was advised to have his daughter tested too, but he did not.

***

The girl was tall for her age, and strong---stronger than most of her contemporaries. At high school she shone at both basketball and softball; she overheard one of the teachers say to another that she could have made the district age team in either sport.

Some of the other girls in her class had developed breasts, and were wearing bras, and they chattered and laughed about things she knew nothing of, fashions and parties and boys. She felt out of place amongst them, and none made any attempt to make her feel welcome. She guessed they probably laughed at her behind her back, at her looks and her country ways. As for the boys, none of them in her class even ever spoke to her.

As she had done in Primary School she befriended one of her teachers. She would spend time with her in the playground at lunchtime, the woman telling her about places she had been and things she had done, and the girl talking about the life she herself knew.

"Don't worry about those other girls," she would later remember Mrs. Holberton saying, "it takes time to make good friends."

***

Although she still walked with her next door neighbour Nigel to the bus stop, she virtually never saw him during school hours. He had grown tall; at fifteen he was a hundred and eighty centimetres.

On weekends, between milkings---and if she could get away--- she still went for rides on her pushbike. In the hope Nigel might accompany her she would call in at his farm, and occasionally he did go. Though they never talked a lot, they were precious times for her---away from her father and the farm and work---just pedalling beside her friend along the quiet little back roads that ran between the dairy farms.

***

When Nigel was due to enter his fourth year at high school his parents decided to send him to boarding school in Melbourne. She hardly ever saw him after that, and if she did bicycle to his place on weekends when she knew he was home from Melbourne, he now always seemed to have other things he wanted to do. She saw he was changing a lot---taller still, and broader in the shoulders, and more muscular. Her own body was changing too.

***

At the end of his first year at boarding school, in the Christmas holidays, Nigel brought another student home with him. When the girl cycled to the Pattinson's on the first weekend of those holidays she did not know they had a visitor.

She saw no-one when she reached the top of their driveway but parked her bike and walked into the barn because she could hear some activity there; she saw a stranger shovelling oats into bags. The boy told her who he was and she told him about being a friend of Nigel's and living on the next door farm. While she was saying this, the boy moved closer to her---and she had a flash of insight about what might be about to happen. When he reached her he put his arm around her waist.

She felt helpless as the boy's arm encircled her, and when he bent and kissed her, first on the cheek and then quickly on the mouth. When he took her hand and pulled her towards a pile of loose hay in a corner of the barn, she did make an attempt to shake her hand free, but the boy's grip was firm. He seemed so confident that she could think of nothing to do or say. Whatever may have been about to happen seemed to be out of her control.

When they were seated side-by-side on the hay, he put a hand on her breast. She tried to pull away then, but he leant over her and once again kissed her on the lips. She struggled but the boy was strong, and now she felt his hand go down the outside of her leg. She called out for him to stop but he kept on, his hand now lifting the hem of her dress and beginning to slide upwards. With all her strength she attempted to roll away but the boy was pinning her to the floor of the barn with his own body. She flailed out with her legs and hit him with her hands---and was suddenly free.

Nigel had arrived, and had hauled his school friend off her. He began punching him; she called out for him to stop, but when the boy began to punch Nigel in return she launched herself at the legs of her attacker and knocked him to the floor. The boy got to his feet and ran out of the barn. The girl, embarrassed, muttered a thank you to her friend and raced to her bike. She learned later that Nigel's parents had put the boy on a bus to Melbourne that same night.

Nigel never mentioned the incident---ever---and neither did she, but it started a train of thought for her, a fantasy in which Nigel became her boy friend. And that seemed so logical. Hadn't they been friends for years? And had he not defended her?

This dream was constantly with her; whenever she felt a little down she took comfort from imagining their future lives together.

***

By the time she was seventeen and finishing high school her father was so debilitated that he was capable of doing almost nothing. She became a full time farmer---up by five every morning and still busy after dark, seven days a week. The father decided only now to tell her that the disease he had was heritable; she had tests done, and they showed that she too was likely to develop the condition in time.

***

She tried to find an hour in the middle of the day for herself---to read or listen to music--- but there were so many things to do on the farm that she hardly ever managed it. And there were the house and the garden to keep in order, and increasingly, her father to care for.

Almost the only relief she got from work on the farm was when she bicycled up to the Pattinson's. Nigel was now at university, and scarcely ever came home, but she would spend an hour with his mother. She liked the woman very much---a woman of energy and humour---lively company. She realised the only time she ever heard laughter---the only time *she* ever laughed---was when she was with her.

Mrs. Pattinson was the only person she ever shared 'girl talk' with---about hair styles and make-up and clothes. They even had a fashion parade one day in the lounge room, Mrs. Pattinson pulling out dress-up clothes that she no longer wore. She had a ball-gown she had last worn ten years before and she insisted the girl try it on. It was a strapless dress and it fitted the girl perfectly. The woman raved about how great the girl looked in it. "You have a great figure---great top. You'd knock the boys dead in something like that." But she was never free to go to dances or balls.

The woman told her that it used to worry her that she was being expected to work on the farm when she was so young. "You won't know this but your teacher asked me if I thought you were being properly treated---or, you know, being exploited. I called in during afternoon milking some times, do you remember? I was just checking that you weren't being asked to do too much. And that you were safe---you know, with the machinery. You were so little."

Mrs. Pattinson also confided, when they were talking about Nigel one day, that she hoped he and she might become more than friends. "I'd love to have you for a daughter-in-law." The girl was too embarrassed to admit that she harboured the same dream.

***

One Saturday when she knew Nigel was due home from university for the weekend, the girl, by then eighteen, bicycled to the Pattinson's. Mrs. Patttinson was talking to a girl in the garden--- tall, slim and quite beautiful. As introductions were being made Nigel came out of the house, walked over and stood next to the newcomer, putting his arm around her waist. He said they were engaged.

She did not stay long, and on her ride back home her feelings gave way to grief; she had invested so much in her 'plan' for Nigel and herself. She sobbed for hours, and in the following days she frequently gave way to tears.

When the crying was through, she forced herself to face the new truth, that the one hope she had nurtured for a happy future---sharing her life with Nigel---would not come about. Could never happen. She would have her father to look after until he died from his condition, a father that she had to admit had never shown her much affection---not the sort of affection she had seen other parents show their children. And then---after his death---what? Farm work, and the likelihood that she herself would develop the same condition. For the first time in her life she questioned the point of living.

***

Her father became so weak that he had to be admitted to a care institution in the town where she had attended high school. His health deteriorated even more quickly there, as doctors had told her it would, and he died within another six months.

The young woman, as his sole beneficiary, was now a property owner. The farm was large and valuable, with big water rights, but it was producing well below what it could; there needed to be a more efficient milking shed---a herringbone, like the Pattinsons had ---and the pastures needed to be renovated, and laser-levelled for better irrigating---all things that her father had not had the energy or the will to do.

Some people in the district tried to buy the farm, but the young woman could not bring herself to sell at the low prices being offered; she knew the place was potentially much more valuable.

Yet she did not begin any of the improvements the farm needed. She felt flat---defeated; she might as well run it as it was---as her father had done---because in the future she would be weak and useless too.

If Nigel had only returned her affection---if they were to marry ---what couldn't they achieve before that happened! She believed they could turn the place into an example to the whole district---a showpiece. But, more than that, the two of them would be partners ---loving partners. For twenty or perhaps even thirty years they could work side-by-side, achieving so much. And be happy.

But that dream had been dashed; instead she felt she was becoming a drudge. She hardly ever left the farm now---a quick trip once a week into the local town's supermarket and that was all. She stopped going to the church she had attended with her father, she never went to any social event in the town or the district, and she now hardly ever even called to see Mrs.Pattinson. She came to see herself as no more than a slave to the farm.

Other women in the district did ask her to visit---to come to Sunday dinner for instance---but she always said that she could not 'get away'. They tried to encourage her to come to tennis afternoons and parties, or to join with them at a dance, but she always declined. And attempts at matchmaking---with a visiting cousin or friend ---failed; any meetings that did take place always became too awkward for all parties, and soon people gave up. "She'll end up an old maid" they told each other.

She consulted doctors again; more tests were done. She was informed that there was a possibility she would not develop the dystrophy---but she put little store by that view. They also said that even if the condition manifested itself, it might not do so until much later in her life. She supposed that the doctors thought that this was an encouraging prognosis, but she did not see it that way; it just meant that she would have to live longer with that cloud over her head. Better an early death than that, she thought---and she actually began to turn her mind to achieving that exit. What if she were to take her own life---and before any symptoms appeared? Would she have the courage to do that? She believed she would---and wouldn't it be better to go when she was still young and strong?

She thought about it often, and by the time she had reached twenty she had so settled on the scenario that it now seemed inevitable. And she was not unhappy about it. What would she miss by leaving this life early? Where was the happiness in it anyhow? And with no relatives, and no close friends, who would mourn her? She decided she would do it when she turned twenty-one.

***

She knew she had to plan for the eventuality in detail. She appointed the Public Trustee as her Executor and had a will drawn up, leaving her estate to a number of charities that she thought did good work.

She would not want to place a burden on her neighbours come the time; she knew their immediate practical concern would be the welfare of her animals. Her birthday was in July, and at that time of the year she always had all the cows dried off, to give them a rest till calving again in the Spring, so at least people would not have to attend to milking them.

There would be no calves to feed, and she would have earlier disposed of any pigs and poultry; she had no pets. The day before her birthday she would put the cows into Willows, the big central paddock of the farm, which she would have left empty for months beforehand, so that there would be plenty of grass there. The paddock had a big natural dam in it which she would make sure was full, so there would be no the risk of the animals running out of drinking water. She would make sure the fences around it were in good order.

***

She would take poison, the odourless and tasteless powder that she got from the vet's for killing rabbits. There would be some pain, but death would be swift.

The day before, she would put notes in the roadside letterboxes of the Pattinsons and two of the other neighbours, asking them to come the next afternoon to the milking shed---where she would have taken her life earlier in the day.

***

On the morning of her twenty-first birthday she checked the cows one last time in their paddock, walking amongst them. The friendlier ones came up to her, as they usually did, and she gave them a scratch, and whispered goodbye. She walked to the milking shed, put a large glass of water on the little table that stood just inside the shed, and took the packet of poison down from a locker. There was a mirror on the wall above the table and she looked at herself one last time. She reached for the white powder.

***

Patricia sipped her drink and leaned back in her lounge chair. She was silent, giving no indication that she was going to complete her story, but I caught a challenge in her look---a challenge for me to do it. I was reluctant, because the ending that seemed most obvious to me was so sad and awful, but there was a serenity in her demeanour that caused a thought to flicker into life.

"She didn't take the poison," I said. "She went on to become the many times re-elected mayor of a northern Victorian Shire."

"I couldn't do it. All of a sudden it came me---what I could do with the rest of my life---for good. I mean, to do good. To help others less fortunate."

"But you had this condition! You yourself were very unfortunate."

"So I thought, but, as you see, it hasn't manifested itself. And the breaking news is that because it hasn't shown up by now, it probably won't. But even if it does...." and she shrugged, and made a dismissive gesture.

"You know, I looked at that little bag of white powder for a long time. And the longer I looked at it the more ridiculous my plan seemed. I had spiralled down in self pity over the years and now as I sat there I realised I just had to spiral back up."

"How did you manage to do that?"

"The old way---counting my blessings. I was young---I was still healthy---I owned and ran a large farm, but that didn't mean I had to remain a slave to it---that could change. And I knew I had a brain, and I could use it."

"What did you do first? Oh---those notes to the neighbours!"

She laughed. "I rang the three neighbours and spun a story about having thought I would need a hand to shift something heavy in the shed but had changed my mind. And then I went down to the paddock where I had put the cows and I walked amongst them again---my friends---almost my only friends at that time. I sang, would you believe; Julie Andrews doing "The irrigation flats are alive......

I cried too, but I was joyous; it was a feeling I don't think I had ever had before."

***

She said she went to her bank and borrowed money. She built a new shed, and then did all the other things the farm needed---renovating the pastures, improving the irrigation layout and fertilising the land. It responded by producing so much more grass she had to buy more cows. Within two years the farm's income had almost doubled.

The following year, when a neighbour decided to retire and sell up, she bought his farm. She purchased another farm a year later; she had to borrow substantially more this time but her management of the existing loans had so impressed the bank that the money was made available very readily.

"I started accepting invitations from my neighbours. I went to socials and parties. I went to dances. I even had boyfriends---though I thought I probably wouldn't ever marry; I was not yet being affected by the condition that took my father, but I knew---believed ---that it was just a matter of time, and I couldn't pass that on to children. I suppose if I had met someone who I thought *would* have been happy for us to share our lives without having children I would have married him---but that never happened."

"A pity."

She nodded."Anyhow I went onto the local Dairyfarmer's committee---went to conferences---and got voted onto the board of the Co-op here. I'd already found share-farmers for the those first two farms but I was now spending so much time away from the home place that I had to put a share-famer on there too. I moved into a house here in town---and before I knew it I was on the Shire Council."

"And then Mayor." I said. " And re-elected every time afterwards."

"Yes, but I've loved it. The first twenty years of my life I hardly knew anyone. Now I know everyone."

"And---I have heard---you help kids."

"I do. The kids I'll never have."

***

After I returned home to work up my copy, it was that story she had shared with me of her early life that stayed with me. I was not free to publish it but I did type it up, and when I went back a fortnight later to check some facts for my newspaper article, I gave it to her to read.

After she read it, she looked at me in that way which she has made her own---straight and calm---a look as if to say 'all things are under control'. It is to my mind a unique look---and I very much like it; it too had stayed with me over the previous fortnight.

"It's strange---it's like reading about someone else now."

"Well---she was."

***

I want to get to know this woman better, and now I will have the opportunity to meet her fairly often. I hope she will welcome this new friendship; I'm beginning to hope it will be a friendship that can become something more.

SEVEN

GOING TO TOWN

The back bar of Brisbane's "Criterion" is busy. A stranger would notice that most of the men are youngish, stylishly dressed and very well groomed. This particular afternoon, nearly all the men in the bar are crowded around the billiard tables.

All four are in use, and if a visitor had been able to get to the front of the crowd, he would have seen that at each of them an *elderly woman* is playing. He would also have seen that each of these women is beating her competitor soundly, in clinical demolitions that are eliciting applause. At the end of the game on each table the woman shakes hands with her opponent and then takes on another of the men.

One of the women, when asked by a man why he has never seen them there before, explains that they live up the coast, and are only in the city for their great-niece's wedding.

***

Melba, Minerva, Harriet and Lily are sisters and widows, all born in the 1920s, and all now living on the same small farm two hours north of Brisbane that was originally bought by their father.

"Camelot" was passed to them and their two brothers when he died, and though by then they all lived elsewhere, and had their own homes, the four women couldn't bring themselves to sell their childhood home, and they leased the land to neighbouring farmers. The women and their husbands took holidays there from time to time over the years.

Because their two brothers had both built up big businesses elsewhere and were now wealthy, and because they could see their sisters were unhappy about parting with the property, they eventually deeded their shares in "Camelot" to them.

The first sister to be widowed asked the others if they would agree to her coming back to their childhood home. When another became a widow she too decided she would move back; eventually all four were living there together---together but not quite, each of the last three building her own house on the land.

***

After I became engaged to Tamara, she took me up there from Brisbane to introduce me to her great aunts. Our visit lasted only twenty-four hours, but it took us---me anyhow---several days at home to get over it. That visit was exhausting; the women always had things they wanted us to see and do, and when we were not indulging them, we were indulging ourselves---in food.

I swear I ate as much in those twenty-four hours as I would in a week at home. We stayed in the old original home with the eldest, Melba, but we ate in all four houses in turn, and it was an endless round of lunches and dinners and afternoon and morning teas. It is no good anyone saying that we did not *have* to eat so much; for one thing, all four were magic cooks, so everything looked tempting and tasted superb, and for another---well, I can only say there is this atmosphere at "Camelot" which takes one over.

In addition to the food, there is the *liveliness* of the four women. Their conversation is high-powered, right up-to-date on world events and issues and trends---and they have *opinions*. I can say that not only does one's stomach get a workout on "Camelot' but one's mind also.

And then there is the billiard table. Just beside the original house is a shed that was once a double garage but now houses a full-sized table, with shaded lights above it, and two rows of banked seats on either side. On the wall there is a rack for cues, and a big scoring board. It is *professional*.

We were obliged to adjourn to it after dinner. I am a mug player ---Tamara a little better than me, courtesy of visits as a child to Camelot---so we each teamed up with one of the women. That left two of them to also pair up; they had to accept a colossal handicap, but they still won.

It must have crossed the minds of the old ones that they had somehow failed in their guidance of their great-niece, else how could she have contemplated, even for a moment, marriage to someone as incompetent at such a vital activity? But they held their tongues, and though they were probably exchanging looks of disbelief and disgust, they must have been very discreet about it, because I never detected any.

They were frighteningly good. They knew what they intended each ball to do---what it *would* do---before they hit it. And they struck those balls so hard you would think they were trying to smash them. These women are in their late eighties and early nineties, but any perception they may have of themselves as 'old ladies' surely deserts them when they enter that shed. They snap on these eyeshades---I swear---and move around the table as energetically as teenagers, and with great purpose; you learn, if it's not your turn, to keep out of their way.

It is not just I who was---is---impressed. They often hold 'open nights', when anyone from the district can turn up and challenge them, and my wife tells me these old dolls nearly always win. It is such a good set up that retired professionals, who do those tours around the country, book it---I believe it's the only time the women lose---but I'll bet they put up a good fight.

The episode later at the Criterieon when they came down for our wedding was totally in character.

***

The women arrived in Brisbane in a limousine, the vehicle and the driver provided by an old friend of theirs who serviced some of the up-market hotels and resorts on the Sunshine Coast. The wedding was to be on a Saturday, in the afternoon, but they arrived on the Thursday because two of them needed outfits.

They went first to their motel in Fortitude Valley, booked by Tammie because it was just a short walk from the church. After they unpacked, they were taken by their driver to the Queen Street Mall in the city centre; they were there by twelve.

Apparently they walked the length of the Mall, calling at virtually every dress shop. Eventually they found a boutique that seemed to have things suitable for ladies of very mature years. What followed must have been an epic of dressing and undressing, and walking up and down and looking in mirrors and asking opinions of sisters and shop assistants and even other customers. The owner, they later told us, handled it all with good humour---good humour no doubt fostered by the realisation that before the afternoon was over she would be pocketing some serious money, all four in fact having decided to buy.

By closing time final decisions had been made, but many alterations were needed; could the owner possibly have them done by the following midday? That wise woman had already alerted her back-up seamstresses; she said they would work through the night if necessary.

The four went back to the motel, and although they had earlier decided they would go out for dinner they were now unanimous that they were all too tired; they ate in their rooms and had an early night. The next morning they were to be ferried back into the city centre to collect their new finery. After that they might think of something else to do; what they would end up doing was those men at the "Criterion".

***

Friends who attended our wedding said that what they remembered most about it was these old women, and I'm not surprised. All four gave entertaining speeches about my wife---embarrassing her appropriately---and then one of them discovered a pianola in a little room off the hall. She found a box of rolls too, and started playing them. With our permission and with the help of several younger guests they pushed the instrument through the door and onto the edge of the dance floor.

The music rolls were of dance tunes but definitely Old Time---waltzes and Gypsy Tap and Pride of Erin and the like; the younger guests did not know the steps but the aunts demonstrated. Soon there was a big circle around the perimeter of the floor, with one or other of the aunts pumping the pedals; when the kids realised that that was all there was to it they took over.

We had hired a DJ for the night, an old school friend of mine, and I went over to him to sort of apologise, but he was cool with it; from then on the 'entertainment' alternated between disco dance music and old-time. It was all good.

***

It had been as the women were returning from Queen Street on the Friday that they had noticed the Criterion, just two blocks before their motel. When the manager of the motel told them the Cri had not one but four tables, the die was cast.

***

When I gathered them up there later that afternoon, the patrons formed a sort of guard of honour, and applauded; while we were strolling back to their motel the four were on a real high.

"Those men were very nice," said Harriet.

"So polite" said Lily.

"Very well dressed," said Minerva.

I asked if they realised the character of the Criterion, and the nature of its clientele. Melba favoured me with the sort of smile one might bestow on a member of one's family who was perhaps a little slow of understanding.

"Of course dear."

EIGHT

BOILERS

She could see something white moving towards her in the long grass below the garden. She settled herself on the old fallen Yellow Box and waited; she was fairly sure that she was about to be presented with gifts. She wondered how many there would be; Veronica was old, so perhaps there might be only one or two.

She leaned back, bracing herself with her hands against the smooth timber, its bark long weathered away. Roy flopped at her feet. The log had been his kennel for years---the hollow end of it---when he was younger, and Andy was alive. Now it was only the hens that used it, scratching around inside it the way they did. One or other of her girls tried to be clever sometimes and start laying a clutch in there. Well, she was too experienced for that---it was one of the first places she looked if one of them went awol.

Since Andy had gone she had allowed the old Blue Heeler to live up on her back verandah; he had his own box, with a few old blankets for warmth in winter. She believed he liked being closer to her. Dogs were pack animals she knew, and while Andy was alive he had been the leader of Roy's pack. She supposed *she* was now; she had only to murmur his name and he was there---a good old friend. "And here's another friend. Oh, eight! Goodness, well done Ronnie."

The trek towards her through the thick grass must have been hard for the little ones---must have seemed like a jungle to them. She wondered where Veronica had had her nest. Surely not that other log right down near the creek?

The chicks clustered around their mother, who had positioned herself right beside Roy; well, none of her girls were frightened of him. She wondered if they realised that, when they were out in the garden. he was always guarding them?

She pulled a handful of chick feed from her apron pocket and threw it at the hen's feet, and the bird did the urgent quiet clucking sound that seemed to mean 'here's food kids'. How often had she heard that?

She marvelled again at how tough new-born things were. She'd seen calves, separated from their mothers when they were only a day or two old, yet still full of the will to live after a week on their own. And the babies of wild wood ducks, still just little balls of fluff, but launching themselves into the air from their nest perhaps fifteen metres up a tree, called down by their mother on the ground.

The first time she had seen that, pointed out by her husband, she could scarcely believe it. None of the ducklings were injured though; one after the other they'd flopped to earth beside their mother but immediately got to their feet and shook themselves, looking perfectly alright, and when the mother had them all, she led them off. Where did she take them? Somewhere near water she supposed---they'd be safer there from foxes or goannas. And how did she know when she had them *all*? Did she count them? Surely she couldn't *know* them, as she herself had known her own babies? When she thought about it, human babies were tough too---if they were healthy.

She would have thought that this hen was too old to lay fertile eggs ---and then hatching out a clutch of eight! What was she---five? No, six---same age as Vanity. She might need some help though to rear this lot.

"You know, you have been very lucky. If a goanna had found your nest you wouldn't have even one chick. Now we'll have to lock you all up at night to be safe." During the day itself they'd be safe enough roaming the garden; no goanna would come anywhere near Roy. "You watch over these little ones." The dog looked up and seemed to understand, and she accepted that he did. She believed that dogs---old dogs---knew much more than people gave them credit for, especially smart dogs like Roy. Kelpies were smart too, but just too 'goey' for her liking; what was that the young people said---like they were on Speed---whatever that was. Border Collies she'd read somewhere were the smartest of all dogs, and she could believe that. Andy could talk to Bess as if she were human. She would love to have had Bess looking after her chooks, back when she was "Emily's Wyandottes", and earning that extra money. Andy had never really understood how much her sales of eggs and chickens had helped them, especially during the droughts.

Roy sat up suddenly. "Yes yes, you're not so wonderful---I can hear it too": in the distance, Bill's Hilux. It was still a few kilometres away, but you could always hear a vehicle as it started to climb the Halifax. Hadn't they had some times getting up that in the early days, before it was bitumened.

She stood and moved towards the house; she'd put the jug on, and if she got going she could have some scones under way by the time Bill arrived. Her nephew would surely stay a while then; everyone loved fresh scones. And he'd have some news. She did hope it was good; she didn't like to think about what it would mean if it wasn't.

He hadn't told her about the specialists he'd been see, in Albury and then in Sydney. His mother had had to tell her that. Well, Diedre would; her sister-in-law and she had always told each other everything. They were as close as real sisters---as close as the brothers they had married had been to each other. Closer really; Andy and Charlie had never been that open with each other. Though they had shared the work of developing the two blocks next to each other---alongside each other day after day and year after year---what they'd told each other personally had had limits.

Bill was a bit of a chip off his father in that way, never saying much to her about himself---about anything really. But he never failed to call in when he was passing, especially since Andy had died, to see if she needed anything he said. He loved her she knew, but he had never even given her a hug. Well, he would get one today---whatever his news.

***

They'd been going on lately about her leaving the farm. Still keeping it of course, but her brother-in-law and his son Bill running it for her, which was more or less what they were doing now, but then she could move to where there were more people. She could come up and live with them if she liked, their house was big enough. They could set it up so she had her own quarters, and could still 'do' for herself. Or---had she thought of one of those retirement villages down the valley in Albury? Only an hour away.

She knew they were only thinking of her. She could have a fall and break something, or she might even have some sort of a turn---a heart attack. How would anyone know? But wasn't there something you could wear now---you just pressed a button and it sent a message?

Her girls were trying to persuade her to live with one of them, in Sydney or Melbourne. Or she could alternate between them. She did like to go to those cities in the train, and stay for a while, but she didn't want to live there. No, and not in one of these 'villages' either; she wanted to stay where she was---in the home she had lived in since she was married. She wanted the familiar things, like the views to the hills to the south, and the valley to the west; she wanted to be able to look from the back verandah over the garden, with her beloved Wyandottes scattered throughout. She would miss all those things too much.

The ute was pulling up as she put the scones into the oven. Thank goodness it wasn't the old slow combustion stove. Even when she had had the thing alight---and she'd very early in her married life realised it was better to keep it going all day rather than let it go out---you never knew when you might need to fire it up suddenly, like now, and it could take another twenty minutes to get it hot enough for scones or bread.

The electricity had only come up to them twenty years ago. Well, they were the last two places on the road, before the State Forest--- but there had been times when she thought it would never arrive. And then it had been heaven, to be able to just flick a switch and have power, instead of having to go down to the shed to start the generator, with Andy all the time going on about not starting it "for any little thing."

Bill's footsteps on the verandah were loud. And confident she thought. Not bad news then. "I've got scones in the oven Bill. Won't be long." She searched his face, but could read nothing. Boys! Was she going to have to dig it out of him? He stood beside the kitchen table---no boy now of course, but a man of almost fifty, healthy looking and strong.

"It's good news Aunt Em. It's benign. They can take it out in Albury." He submitted to the hug.

After he'd gone she went to the back verandah and sat at the top of the steps. Shadows were lengthening; she'd soon have to put her girls away. Girls!? Boilers really, all of them, and she wondered if anyone did still boil up old poultry as her mother used to do--- breaking up the meat afterwards and putting it into pies and bakes. It had been a good way of using old hens that had stopped laying. Not that she would even think of doing that to any of her friends. She was an old boiler herself now she supposed.

A clucking at the bottom of the steps made her look down: Veronica, with her new ones. The woman felt a tenderness towards them; she'd always had a special feeling for the 'illegals'. She tried something now she had never done, persuading a hen to climb the steps. She called quietly.

The bird hopped up onto the first step and then the second, making a different sound that she also knew well---'come to me" The boldest of the chicks made a fluttering leap up onto the first step and then others followed. The hen kept coming---'tuck tuck'---and so did the little ones. Eventually the whole group was on the step beside her feet. She took more chick feed from the pocket of her apron and held it down; the hen pecked some from her hand, and then she sprinkled the rest along the step for the little ones. Roy, beside her as usual, made a small sound---"I'm here too"---and she rested her hand on his head.

Yes, she would stay here. Where else would she hear the sounds a hen made for her babies, and that of a faithful dog when he wanted a pat? And then there were the white cockatoos; you could hear them right across the valley. And the calls of the different parrots; she prided herself that she could identify them all.

She loved to hear Zachariah flap his wings and give his first crow of the morning. She loved the sound of the wind in the gum trees when a squall was approaching, and of course the rain on the iron roof---just about the very best sound.

'You should live your last years where you would like to die,' she had once read, and she thought that was so right. And that would be here---*here*---where she could catch the scent of the first blossoms on the Valencia orange, and, at Christmas time, pick the ripe Elberta peaches. *Here*, where she could stand on her verandah on a crisp winter's morning and feel the first rays of the sun on her skin, and, when there was a full moon, walk in her garden under its pearly light, sometimes, if it was a very warm night---her little secret--- quite naked.

NINE

TAKING A POSITION

As Isobel stood to leave the Director's office, the man told her that he had commissioned a name plate to be put up beside the door of her own office.

"That will be nice, Director." Although her boss addressed staff by name, she had learned that he wished always to be addressed by title.

"Well, 'Curator of Fine Arts' deserves a nice plate. Not quite as nice as mine of course," with a chuckle.

But when the plate arrived it read ' Isobel Jelly', though she had been divorced for several months, and had told everyone, including him, that she now wished to be known by her maiden name, Isobel Jones.

"But dear lady, I understand that the final papers have not yet been issued?"

"Yes, some admin hitch....." How did he know that? "But it is final. I am divorced."

"Well...." and he shrugged, and his hands came up from the desk, the fingers fanned out----a 'what can I do' gesture with which she would become quite familiar in the coming months---"I'm afraid until those final papers come through it is proper that you remain Mrs. Jelly. I believe I have to take that position."

It was the first of what would be several ongoing frustrations for her in her new job.

***

She knew her appointment as Curator of Fine Arts at the State Gallery had been generally approved of in the arts world. She was already Director of the city's biggest private gallery, with a high profile, not just in that city but throughout the whole Australian arts world. She prided herself on having a wide knowledge of all the arts, and of their histories. She did have a special interest in porcelain, and had her own large collection.

There had been many applicants for the State's Curator position, including the person who had been filling the role temporarily, the Gallery's own Assistant Curator (Porcelain and Glass) Darcy De Montville. The short list had eventually come down to just De Montville and herself. The man had been placed there by the Director himself, and in her interview with the Director she felt his manner was somewhat hostile towards her; she came to the conclusion that he very much wanted his own man to continue in the position.

When finally both De Montville and she had faced the full placement panel together---two directors of other metropolitan art galleries, 'her' Director and two members of his Board---she observed that any questions the Director put to De Montville were light ones---almost 'Dorothy Dixers'---whereas the questions he put to her were tougher, and capable of a range of answers; the man would then seem to take issue with whichever answer she did give. This had worried her, but after a while she sensed that it was not influencing the other members of the panel.

When her appointment had been confirmed, she knew that she still had the task of winning the Director around, and, possibly more difficult, the passed-over one himself; she was now his immediate superior.

***

The nameplate issue proved to be just the Director's first strike--- that, and the fact that he persisted in introducing her to visitors as "Mrs. Jelly" It seemed to her he emphasized the 'Mrs', in a way that, to her ears, made the word sound 'domestic' and even silly, out of keeping with the position and its surroundings.

"I know I shouldn't fuss about it but---it's getting to me" she said to Grant, her ex-husband, when they were having coffee together in the Gallery café.

"There's something wrong with the man," was his opinion.

***

The divorce papers came through and a new nameplate was installed---but by then the Director had found other weapons.

When prominent arts people visited the gallery, she found she was being kept out of the loop. She and other senior staff *were* receiving emails about the visitors, but she also would have expected to be invited to meet them. She understood that the subjects of the meetings might well have been about matters that did not immediately concern her, but the man was flouting a rule generally followed in the world of big public art galleries---that high-level visits always extended to at least a greeting of other senior staff members. It was not only polite but useful in future dealings, and networking was something on which she prided herself.

***

The two offices of the Director and herself were on the first floor, that of the Director on one side of the building, with a view over the city, hers on the other, somewhat smaller but with a view over the river and to the mountains fifty kilometres away. (She thought it had much the nicer outlook.)

The open area in the centre of the building between them was used for special exhibitions. It was when she was passing through this area that Isobel, by accident, sometimes saw these visitors. She was thinking she would eventually raise the issue with her boss.

Then, when she had been in the job for some three months, she saw a new poster in the ground floor foyer announcing a forthcoming exhibition of Scandinavian glassware---a top event. Why had she not been informed of this?

Oh, the man said, it had been arranged months before by De Montville---before she had taken on the job; he hadn't wanted to bother her with it. She let him know that she *wanted* to be 'bothered' with such things. She asked who was going to open it or talk about it and he said it would be De Montville.

***

As part of her job she was obliged to attend meetings of the Board; at one of the early ones there was an item on the agenda regarding progress in an approach to Tokyo for a loan of porcelain. She asked such basic questions about it that the Chairman asked if she had been appraised of it. She said she had not, and that as Curator of Fine Arts, she should have been. The Board agreed, and postponed the discussion.

After the meeting the Director said that there needed to be 'better communication' between the two of them, seemingly suggesting that any fault in that regard had been on her side.

***

There were other niggles. During meetings between the two of them in the man's office, he accepted all phone calls, but she soon saw that most of the calls were unimportant, often of a merely social nature, and ones that could easily have been returned later; some of the conversations went on for many minutes. He had a habit of looking at her while talking with a caller; I rate this person more highly than I do you, he might well have been saying.

She tried showing her irritation by looking at her watch very obviously, but this had had no effect. On perhaps the tenth occasion it occurred, she scribbled a note---'in my office'---and walked out. She had barely reached her office when he rang and asked her to come back. He remonstrated with her---'I would have been only a minute'---but she reminded him that such calls had previously lasted many minutes, and in any case, she couldn't help noticing that most of them were of no great moment.

He had stood on his authority; the Director must decide which calls he would take, and when. She said of course, Director, but meanwhile she should be getting on with her own work.

That problem ceased---but others persisted. Many arranged meetings did not take place, and were cancelled at very short notice, even ones for which she had sometimes done, at his request, a great deal of preparation. All she would be told by his secretary was "the Director is sorry but he has had to cancel your meeting." She made a list of the cancelled meetings, some eleven of them in a period of just two months, and then brought the matter up.

"My dear lady, in this job there is so much…..", waving his hand over his calendar and diaries, as if to indicate the extent of the demands on his time, but she had placed the list on the desk in front of him. The cancellations ceased.

Then there was his habit of entering her office without appointment, even without knocking, as if whatever she was doing could safely be interrupted at his whim. Even when she was having an important discussion, with an overseas dealer or a possible donor, and he had been informed of this through his secretary, he would still enter. He was 'The Director'---no doors were to be barred to him.

Sometimes he would have other people with him, "to show them the view" he would say, but she suspected it was primarily to reinforce his authority---and possibly to shake her confidence in her hold on the job.

***

She thought that if perhaps the two of them could get to know each other socially, his attitude might change. She invited him to a small dinner party one weekend. He would have been delighted, he said, but he would be away that weekend. The next Saturday? Unfortunately he had a prior engagement.

All her invitations proved 'impossible'; she faced the fact that the man did not want to come---did not want any thaw in their relationship.

***

She had a problem with the passed-over De Montville as well; she was having to work with him almost daily, but was finding him very prickly. If she questioned some suggestion or proposal of his, he seemed to take it personally; it became difficult to discuss anything with him.

She brought the situation out into the open one day, while they were having coffee in her office and he had made what she considered an unhelpful remark. She said look, we both applied for this job, I got it, but now we both need to move on; let's try and work with each other shall we.

The man had nodded, and she would have pursued the subject, but for the fact that the man appeared as though he were about to break down in tears.

The relationship between De Montville and the Director seemed to remain close. The Assistant Curator seemed to have unfettered access to the Director's office, and the two were often seen together in different parts of the gallery.

Her secretary, a woman with whom she was working well, told her there was gossip that they were lovers, but Isobel gave that no weight---thought it was not something that she should even have to think about. Neither did she dwell on the news from an old colleague that the man with the aristocratic sounding name had had a more 'ordinary' name until his mid twenties.

She asked De Montville himself to a dinner party at her home and he did accept. During the dinner he talked a lot, showing off his knowledge somewhat she thought, but seeming to enjoy the evening. He praised her collection of porcelain. On the Monday morning there were flowers on her desk and a thank you note, and she hoped that the effort had been worthwhile, and that they might now be able to work together more harmoniously, but in the canteen she overheard him telling another of a hilarious dinner party he had attended---and of the ignorance and poor taste of some of the other guests---and she realized it was her dinner.

Even the Director brought it up, saying that Darcy had told him what a delightful evening it had been, but looking at her with such malicious good humour that she was sure he had had the full benefit of De Montville's 'take'.

***

Finally she admitted to herself that she had in them two implacable enemies. It was making her work harder, and far less pleasant than she had hoped it would be. Her ex-husband said that her position was in danger, but she was not to worry because as a lawyer with good contacts in the building industry he felt sure he could arrange for a couple of 'associates' to visit either or both of the gentlemen. At home, at night. He assured Isobel that such visits had straightened out far more recalcitrant problems in the building industry. "No violence of course. Just---an understanding." She declined the offer, but with some regret.

Grant predicted that one of two things would happen; she would make some slip-up and the Director would use that to discredit her, or the assistant curator would bring off some coup which would elevate him.

***

The man proved prescient. One morning she read in the paper that the State Gallery had brought off 'the acquisition of the century'; the famous Gaude vases had been located and purchased, at a cost of five million dollars, through a special grant from the Federal Government. Art commentators around Australia were hailing the purchase. The Director was quoted as saying that he had already received a bid from an overseas gallery at fifty percent more than they had paid. He gave every credit for the purchase to his "enterprising" Assistant Curator Darcy De Montville.

She knew quite a lot about the Gaude, a single set of five porcelain vases made in the early nineteenth century. The suite, graduated in size and featuring birds in the decorations, had been a sensation from the moment they appeared---exquisite in both design and realisation---but it had disappeared into private ownership in the early nineteen-hundreds.

While she had been studying at the Sorbonne she had begun collecting porcelain, originals by choice, but if she saw a very good reproduction of a notable piece she bought that too. She had acquired a copy of the Gaude "Waterbirds".

***

She rang the Director at his home, congratulating him and asking for an appointment that morning. He said he would be busy all day but she insisted. "I must be briefed on this purchase. What if one of the Board members rings me to ask about it?" She realized afterwards that that was probably exactly what the man was hoping; the less she knew about the negotiations and the purchase, the more likely it was that Board members might think she was not on top of her job.

When she arrived at work she told her secretary that she would not be available to anyone until after she had her meeting with the Director in the late morning. Though she was angry at having been kept in the dark, she decided she would not show it. At the meeting with the Director she would be impressed, and generous in her praise, both of him and his---their---subordinate.

At the meeting however she found she had to struggle to keep her temper because of the man's manner. He gave only the most perfunctory answers to her questions about the negotiations, and the research that De Montville had done.

She knew she could not let this pass. She said that she should have been kept in the loop---that the correct course would have been for De Montville to inform her first, and for her to have been involved in the purchase. At this, the Director waved his hand dismissively.

"Procedures---protocols. My dear lady, of what importance are such things when a trusted employee comes to me with such an opportunity?"

"But why did he not come to *me*? He knows my special field is nineteenth century French porcelain. He has been to my home and seen my copy of one of the Gaude vases."

"Well, that is something you will have to ask yourself."

"And him."

"And, as you say, him. Though I must warn you that any disciplinary action that you feel inclined to take---well, it should be kept in perspective against the very real benefits his initiative has bestowed on this place." He leaned back in his chair, and she was reminded of her husband's warning; 'gotcha' was written large across his face.

As she left his office, the Director reached for his phone, and she was not surprised to learn, when she arrived at De Montville's office, to be told that the man was "engaged". She stalked back to her own office, and told her secretary she was not to be disturbed except for the most urgent or important matter.

***

She realised she was in an bad position. If she let people know she had not been included in the negotiations, it would look as if the Director had not had confidence in her---and neither had her subordinate---but if she did anything other than speak positively and indeed praisingly about the acquisition and the work of De Montville, she could appear small-minded and jealous.

Looking beyond that, she could see that it put her hold on the job at risk. In six months her two year contract would be up. If De Montville re-applied---and she was now certain that would happen ---he would have this very recent and spectacular coup on his CV. It was the sort of thing that counted very heavily with selection panels.

The Director had already shown that he favoured the man over her; now this could become his decisive weapon.

***

The vases arrived from Switzerland a week later and were placed in the vaults while a new exhibition cabinet was being constructed. The Director had decided that the cabinet would be placed on their floor, close to his office.

Isobel went with the Director to look at the vases in the vault. The set was graduated in size: "Songbirds" at twenty centimeters high, "Waterbirds" at thirty, "Birds of the Forest" at forty, "Birds of the Plains" at fifty and "Birds of Prey" at sixty. Even in that stark environment and under harsh fluorescent lighting, she thought they looked magnificent. She did not touch them, the Director having decreed that no person other than himself could ever handle them, for fear of damage; "if anybody's head must roll it shall be mine".

***

De Montville told her that he had received a tip from an old university friend, who lived now in London, that the set might be on the market. De Montville, during a short holiday, had gone to Switzerland, and while there had managed to get himself invited to a party that was to be attended by the owner of the vases. De Montville had introduced himself and had secured an invitation to the man's home---a chateau---to see them. During the inspection, the man confirmed that he was considering putting them onto the market; despite the appearance of wealth, the man had apparently suffered big losses in an insurance crash, and these were his most valuable saleable assets.

De Montville had asked the man if he minded where the vases went and he had said no, so long as they could be viewed by the public. De Montville had returned home, consulted with the Director, and with his approval had asked his friend in London to begin negotiations.

De Montville assured Isobel that he had had the vases authenticated, by two of the world's experts in European porcelain.

***

The vases were placed in their new display cabinet with great ceremony. The whole Board was present, plus the Premier and the media. The Director made a speech and in it he praised "our young and brilliant assistant curator, Darcy De Montville." He graciously yielded the floor to his junior, who also made a speech. Board members lined up to shake his hand.

Isobel had offered to also talk, about the design and workmanship, and about the place of the vases in the history and development of porcelain, but the Director had turned her down. She still attended but stood back; when someone asked her to comment she was positive and full of praise, for the vases and the man who had secured them.

***

Whenever Isobel walked across the wide space between her office and the Director's, she would see people gathered at the new exhibits. She too also frequently stopped. She took a particular interest in 'Waterbirds', and came to the conclusion that she owned a very fine copy indeed; without seeing the original and her Carotto copy side by side she really couldn't see any difference. She *would*, she felt sure, if she could handle the original, but the Director had issued his edict on that matter.

On more than one of these occasions, while she was looking at the display, the Director joined with her in silent adoration. Not always silent; he frequently reminded her of De Montville's achievement; "I think there are big things ahead for that young man."

***

Two months after their arrival, the Director came to her and said that he had had advice that they should increase the insurance on the vases to ten million dollars; would she arrange that?

The insurance company asked her for more written evidence of authentication. She told the Director she would need to go through the details of the sale, and to get the history of the vases, as far as it was available---their 'provenance'. He waved his hand dismissively ---whatever she wanted---as though he regarded it all as a bit unnecessary; she felt he had scarcely listened to her.

She called in De Montville and began to ask questions. The man said he'd need to get his notes, and came back shortly after with the contact details of the seller, the two experts who had verified the vases and his friend in England.

It was at this moment Isobel felt the beginnings of doubt. One of the 'experts' was a man whom she had been warned about. People both in Australia and overseas had advised her against having any dealings with him; 'rather too easily influenced by the prospect of a large commission', was how one had put it. The name of the other man was new to her.

She did not recognize the name of the seller but that was not unusual; many very wealthy art patrons were secretive. Over the years some of the most spectacular and valuable objects had emerged from the most unlikely of places.

She first called De Montville's friend in London but found the man guarded. When she asked about the steps in the transaction---who had heard what, who contacted whom first, etc---he too said that he really needed to refer to his notes, and that they were not with him, and that he would get back to her. She thanked him, but said it was a matter of some urgency.

The Director shortly afterwards asked her to come to his office. When she got there she found De Montville too. The Director was barely civil; what exactly did she hope to achieve by talking with Smith in England? She replied that without the information she was seeking, the insurance company would not insure the vases for the greater sum.

"Darcy could have handled all that."

"Yes, but I think the insurance company would not have seen him as a disinterested party."

"What do you mean by that? Are you implying......?"

"Implying nothing, Director." But now she thought---strange that he should leap on that as some sort of accusation. And De Montville himself was looking uncomfortable. Then it came out.

"Look, I've had a talk with Darcy and it seems he---we---may have cut some corners a little. In order to secure the purchase you understand. I've told him he was a bit naughty but I think, under the circumstances---young enthusiastic employee wanting something great for his gallery….."

Young!? The man was only two years younger than she. And exactly what had gone on here?

As she was leaving, the Director walked her to his door---the first time he had ever done that. "I'm sure you appreciate how much hangs on a favourable investigation by you, so if I can help in any way…..

Oh, and something else---that big exhibition in New York next month. I'm just beginning to realise that I have overstretched my schedule. You will have to go, it seems. I hope you like New York?" Beaming now at her---all innocence and goodwill.

"I'm expecting a call from Switzerland in ten minutes Director, from the vendor of the Gaude. That should clear up most of the things the insurance company will need."

As she walked across to her office she realized that these men---men who had made her job more difficult than it need have been---were now nervous, and craving her goodwill. I hope, she thought---God, I hope---there is nothing fishy about this purchase.

***

The man in Switzerland did not call. The operator said that in fact there was no-one of the name listed in Zurich. Anywhere in Switzerland? Nein.

She rang the two "experts"; one was not answering, the other had a recorded message to the effect that the man would be away for an indefinite period. She rang Smith in London again and asked him to try and locate them. She said she needed to hear from him urgently.

When by nine the next morning she had not heard back, she went to the Director's office. She asked his secretary if anyone were with him and when she was told no, she pushed at the door and walked in. The man glared at the intrusion, but she thought she saw more anxiety in his face than anger.

"I need to examine the vases. Myself." He continued to stare. "I have a reasonable doubt that---all is well."

"You don't think......?" He didn't seem able to finish the sentence. His face paled.

"It's possible. And I may not be able to tell. We may have to get Blattner."

"From Germany!?"

She nodded. "Let me have a look first. I have studied Gaude. And you will know I have a good copy of one of his set myself." Which you would have looked at with me, if you hadn't decided that you couldn't possibly cross my threshold.

**

The next day the Director closed the first floor and with two extra security guards on hand unlocked the display cabinet. A table had been set up, covered first with a soft rubber mat and then with felt. Isobel had brought in her own 'Waterbirds', handing it to the Director, who made an identifying mark on the inside of it in blue chalk.

Extra lights were brought and set up, Isobel settled herself in an upright chair, two magnifying glasses were placed on the table beside her, and the Director brought her the smallest vase, 'Songbirds', and laid it on the felt.

Isobel looked at it for a long time without touching it and then with her gloved hand slowly rolled it over. Now she picked up a magnifying glass, and looked particularly at the tails of the birds. She picked up the stronger glass and looked again.

"Thank you. Could I have 'Waterbirds' please?"

"Yes, but----what do you think?"

"It's beautiful. It seems genuine to me."

'Waterbirds' was placed in front of her. This time, as she was using the first of the magnifying glasses, she stiffened and said a soft 'oh'. The Director handed her the larger of the two glasses but she shook her head.

"What?"

"This one is a copy. It's by the same man who made mine. Carlo Carotto."

"How can you tell?"

She moved out of the chair and invited her boss to sit. "Roll the vase until you are looking at the white crane. Look at the fine feathers on the underside of the tail."

He did this and then looked up at her for further guidance.

"Can you see the letters CC?"

"No"

"They are tiny. Just here', and she pointed. He looked again.

"It's Carotto's mark. It's on every one of his pieces. Somewhere. On the Gaudes it's on the tails of the birds. It is on my reproduction so I knew where to look."

The Director checked her copy through the glass, then looked again at the other. After a minute he put the glass down and slowly looked up at her.

"So what do we have?"

"Well I don't know yet. At least one copy anyhow."

The man looked shattered, and she actually felt sympathy for him.

"It may only be the one. We all know of collectors who have all of a set except one and acquire a copy to make it up."

And so it turned out. Isobel, and later the German, confirmed that what the Gallery had purchased were four of the missing Gaudes plus a copy. Not a disaster---but certainly not insurable for ten million dollars and no longer even for five. The most the company would agree to was one million.

***

Darcy De Montville---nee Neville Morton---found himself a position in a regional gallery soon afterwards. When Isobel's contract expired she was automatically re-appointed Curator.

During the following year the Director remained hostile to Isobel but she no longer saw him as a powerful enemy. At the end of the year the man decided that a chronic ailment required him to take his superannuation. Isobel's friends are telling her that the position is hers for the taking.

TEN

WENDY'S PIN

Summer was too hot, she always told people---too hot for her anyway---and winter too cold, and spring, well, it was neither one thing nor the other---you never knew where you were. But autumn---aah, those beautiful sunny days, and nights that were not yet cold, but cool enough for a cheerful fire in the lounge room, cheerful company for a widow.

And what she loved most about autumn, she would say, was the leaves. She knew all the best deciduous trees in her town; there was one avenue of Golden Ash that was just wonderful. It was the trees with the red leaves though that she most admired; the Pistachios were the very best, but many of the Liquidambers put on a great show too, like the ones in her own street, scarlet right through to maroon.

She wished she and Harry had planted more deciduous trees in their own garden when they first moved into the house; the trees she had now were lovely, but they were still only half grown; some of her friends had magnificent specimens. Other friends had only Eucalypts, which she liked well enough, but only out in the countryside; they looked good there she thought, but in the town, no, the deciduous trees were best.

She liked them all---except the Planes. Good shade trees in summer, yes, but they always began to lose their leaves too early, when one still needed the shade, and in any case they didn't turn any sort of colour at all, just going pale and then brown. And on top of that the leaves were so big, and when they clumped together on the ground after rain.....!

She'd written to the Council more than once asking to have them replaced, especially the big ones at the shopping centre; she'd suggested Pin Oaks, or the new Red Maples people were talking about.

***

A Wednesday, Wendy's tennis day, so she would have the two grandchildren as usual. She put any breakables up out of the reach of curious fingers, and set out the little chairs and table in the sun room, with the colouring books and crayons.

She had learned though that colouring books didn't keep little dynamos occupied for very long. She usually took them to the corner park then, where there were swings and a slippery dip, or on a long walk, with Chaffie on a lead. Today she would take them to the main shopping centre, she needed a couple of things, and the girls loved it there; she would treat them again in that food court. She liked to spoil them, they were lovely kids.

***

Though it was sunny, there had been a shower overnight, and a wind from the south-west was beginning to get up; she buttoned up the girls jackets, and insisted they put on the beanies that she kept at the house especially for them. Winter was on its way---though she was sure there would still be time for some more nice weather.

She herself put on a woollen coat and a felt hat, and the three of them stepped out into the wind. She didn't like wind, it always put her on edge.

The hat she was wearing had a wide floppy brim, and they had not even reached her front gate before it blew off. She bustled the girls back inside; she needed a hat pin. She selected one Wendy had given her once as a birthday present, silver and curved, with a polished tawny agate at the end; the agate would go nicely with the hat's emerald green.

***

The wind was really quite cold, and she congratulated herself on covering up the girls and herself so thoroughly. The air was full of leaves too, though she saw that the Claret Ash near the first corner was holding fast to its leaves. All the trees were different in that way, she had noticed; if she were younger and wanted to plant more, she would choose trees like the Ash, ones that resisted winter.

The little ones of course did not notice the wind or the cold. They skipped and danced around her, and when they came to a pile of leaves against a garden fence they ran into them and kicked them up. Well, she had done the same thing at that age.

She allowed them only a few metres of freedom though. She was very careful like that---more careful than their own mother, she had thought more than once---but then she had to be. She wanted her daughter to believe that the children, whenever in Granny's care, could not be in better hands. She prided herself on that.

***

The wind was making such a lot of noise in the trees that she didn't at first hear the car reversing fast up the driveway. She called out urgently for the girls to stop.

The car did slow down before it reached the footpath, and the woman driver smiled, and waved to the three of them, but her heart pounded; it had been the very thing she feared most on these walks.

She felt anxious now, even thought of going back to the house. First the hat, now this---and things always happened in threes, people said. She'd be even more vigilant.

At each street crossing she insisted on holding the children's hands, and repeated to them the rule about looking left and right, and not running across. She thought that actually these two were good in that regard, better than her own daughter had been at the same age, but she couldn't take any risks. How careful would they be if they were on their own and were distracted by something---a dog, or an ice-cream van? What if they saw one of their friends across the street? Would they forget, and just go? She thought they probably would. Well, they were still just babies, really.

***

They were nearing the shopping centre, and the wretched Planes; the wind was tearing their big brown leaves from the branches. Some of them that were already on the ground had stuck together from the overnight rain, but the wind was so strong it was lifting even these pancakes into the air.

And now---skateboarders! Why they seemed to prefer the town centre to the special park the Council had built for them she didn't know; were they just showing off? It was a boy thing she supposed, but when you really looked at them, you realised many of them were as big as men.

They were certainly daring; what she had seen them do on television made her wonder how they didn't kill themselves. And they went so *fast*. She took the girls' hands again; she would need to keep a sharp lookout. Those three things.....

***

At the main intersection, at the town's only traffic lights, she tried to keep the girls on either side of her but they had decided they wanted to hold each other's hands, so while they waited for the

'Walk' signal, both girls were to one side of her, and she had hold of only one little hand.

The girls began to call out, waving to one of their friends on the other side of the street. Another gust blew more Plane leaves into the air. One landed on her shoulder; it was wet, and she let go of the child's hand to brush it off. Then several, stuck together, landed right on top of her hat. She shook her head but the leaves remained there.

She lifted both hands to her head and found why they had not fallen; they were stuck on the hat pin. She bent her head to pull them away, but it took some time, and when she did finally look up again *the girls were in the middle of the road*. She called out to them to come back, but they took no notice, their attention fixed on their friend on the other side.

She was about to follow them when the woman beside her grabbed her arm---and then she too saw the big Council truck coming fast. Those around her shouted to the girls; a woman screamed.

***

She had read that people who observed an accident sometimes said that it seemed to happen in slow motion, and this was how it was for her now. The two girls in the road---the on-coming truck---the agitation of the people near her---all seemed to be part of a dream. But then people were clapping, and miraculously the girls were once again beside her.

"What happened?" She felt dazed. When she looked around she saw people shaking the hand and patting the back of a young man standing nearby, a skateboard in his hand.

"Didn't you see?" a woman asked. "That boy picked them up. As he was coming across. One under each arm! It was amazing."

"He deserves a medal," a man said.

Still dazed, she knelt and hugged the girls, then stood again and turned; she needed to thank the boy, but he was gone.

**

She has never told Wendy about the incident. When her daughter said that the girls had told her about some man giving them a ride on his skateboard, she had passed it off as just a fun thing she had permitted them---but it had been weeks before she had even been able to bring herself to go back to the town centre. She hadn't used Wendy's pin again either. She would one day. One day.

ELEVEN

TAXIS

There's something about taxi drivers that gets to my friend Rodney, and, I have to say, something about Rod that gets to them. Whatever it is, they fight.

Some background here. He and I are both in the theatre game; I write revue material and he has directed a lot of my stuff over the years. We spend a lot of time together and fortunately we get along; he is fun to be with. But he has this streak---this intolerance---of what he calls bullshit. And if you are saying to yourself, that's a good thing---maybe the world needs more Rodneys---I agree, but sometimes I think one should just chill, and let it go. One doesn't have to react every time, or correct every 'wrong' view; sometimes it is better, in my opinion, to just let a thing slide.

Take yesterday. A taxi is at the rank right in front of the "Palmerston", the theatre where our current revue is playing---thankfully to good houses. We slide into the back, and I tell the driver which hotel we're staying at; it's a nice old one about six kilometres away on the foreshore.

The driver is a lean, fit looking man---something of a rarity I have found amongst taxi drivers---and I get an instant feeling he has 'attitude'. While there are drivers who will say nothing, even when one has tried to start a conversation, this one I think has views, and will be keen to put them.

You might ask how I can get that from someone who has not yet uttered a word, and I can only say in my defence that I am a writer, and we writers are observers.

***

"You blokes actors?" Here we go.

"No", I say, "I am a writer and my friend is a director."

"That sounds like easy money."

I silently groan; I am pretty sure he will get Rodney going. I don't really feel like engaging in conversation with the man but I think it will be a more peaceful trip if I do. "Well some would say so, but it's not a steady income; we've both had some lean times."

The driver---I can see from his identification card on the dashboard that his name is Ray---waves his left hand dismissively; he's not having that.

"I see in the paper some guy gets fifty thousand dollars every time for that new television show . Every week!" I think he is referring to an article in the previous day's "Sun" about a Larry Waterson who is the chief writer of an American hit television series and who is visiting here. "I think it's crap."

I am not going to admit to him that I too think it's crap. What I do know is that it is a top rating show in the States, and I suspect it will be here too.

"How come people pay him so much money for stuff like that?"

"It's the market---supply and demand my friend." For the first time my companion speaks up, and there is an edge to his voice that makes me begin to feel sorry for our interrogator.

"How do you mean?"

"That program is rating its arse off on television in the States. So the TV station can charge a lot to advertisers---and pay a lot to the producers who make the program---and they have to keep the writers on that are delivering what the television station will continue paying them big bickies for, and Waterson is the main man."

It is a concise and logical package and the man in front is silenced for a moment. But only a moment.

"But I could write that crap. Anybody could."

"Possibly. So go write something."

"Are you having a go at me?"

"No, I am responding to what you said. You might be able to write better stuff, and you should have a go." And then he adds "but maybe you are just having a bad day?" This last said somewhat lightly---a rising inflection on 'day'; there is just a hint of empathy in Rodney's voice, but Ray is not having empathy either.

"Why do you say that? As a matter of fact I've had a very good day." He puts his hand into his top shirt pocket and, unwisely I think, waves a bulging wallet at us. "I've had some really good fares, from people who work for their money. People who have real jobs."

I feel Rod shift on the seat beside me; I make a decision to be quick to pay for the fare when we arrive. I fear that any argument between these two over the amount, or whether the driver is entitled to keep any change, could prove incendiary.

***

It's not just the drivers who try to 'lecture' him that earn Rod's ire, but any that he thinks are acting badly. On several occasions I've witnessed them have issues over tips.

My friend is actually a generous man; I have seen him give quite large tips, in restaurants and hotels, if the service has been good. But 'ordinary' service gets no tip, and 'inferior' earns words with the manager.

***

I remember one time I was in the back of the cab and Rod was sitting beside the driver---a non-communicative type who had not helped us put our bags into the trunk. Bad move. The fare was not a big one and Rod handed over a twenty dollar note. The man put it in a note clip, reached down and released the trunk latch and sat back; my work's done---goodbye fellas.

I got out and went to the rear to start getting my bags out; Rodney did not appear and so I got his two out also. I put them all together on the pavement outside our hotel and then walked to the driver's door; perhaps he and Rod were having a 'chat'. They were.

"I'm not getting out till you give me my change!"

"Mate---it's a dollar fifty," the man's voice dripping with scorn.

"Perhaps, but it's *my* dollar fifty, not yours."

"Mate---I don't know where you're from, but in this town you tip the cabbie. It's normal."

"Mate"---and you could practically see the sarcasm around the word---"where I come from, which happens to be here, cabbies who do not help us with our baggage do not get a tip."

Our man released a grunt of disgust. As if that were anything to get high and mighty about! He stared defiantly at Rod, but I could have advised him to give up. Rodney would win; Rodney always wins these things.

***

Then there was the time a driver had a CD playing in the cab. Now Rod and I have both travelled overseas quite a lot and we are accustomed to drivers in some countries having their own concert in the front seat, especially drivers in the Middle East. And sometimes it is too loud but I have never made much of a fuss about that. Somehow it's all part of the 'colour' of travel; we theatre types understand all that. But *here*---in this country....?

And don't get me wrong. Neither Rod nor I object to a driver playing something, but quiet enough to allow us to carry on a conversation in the back seat. But this guy had 'Cold Chisel' turned right up; we had heard it when we were approaching the vehicle. I assumed he would turn it down when we got in but no. I leaned forward and tapped the driver on the shoulder.

"Will you turn it down a bit please?" I am a fan of Cold Chisel, but this was too much.

His response was to put his foot to the floor and join the traffic--- and leave the music up loud. I leant over the front seat and shouted- --I had to shout to make myself heard---"will you turn the music down." No please this time.

Half turning his head, he said it was his cab and he would play whatever music he liked and as loud as he liked. Unbelievable. I looked at Rod beside me---to find him grinning---though I didn't think it was funny. Then Rod started rummaging in his little carry- on bag and fished out his own CD player. He switched it on---it already had an early 'Santana' in it---and turned up the volume.

Now this little machine has phenomenal speakers---I think Rod may have had it fiddled with some time---and so began a battle of the sounds. The driver cast an angry glance over his shoulder, reached forward and gave his volume control another turn, whereupon Rod did the same. The noise in that vehicle---you couldn't call it music---was criminally loud. I put my hands over my ears and gave Rod a 'what are you doing?' look, but he had a manic grin that I recognised. Battle had been joined.

At one point the driver looked at me in his rear vision mirror and I grinned at *him*. He must have thought he had a couple of crazies in the back; would he escape with his life?

The duel continued all the way to our destination, thankfully not all that far, but the funny thing is, neither said anything about it when we got there. I looked at the meter, paid the exact money, and the man drove away. And people ask me where I get my ideas for skits.

***

There is that endearing habit some taxi drivers have of speeding away after learning where you would like to go, if the destination is not to their liking. Rod and I long ago learned to stymie that one by piling in first---if we do not have any luggage---and then enlightening the driver. Some of them have become quite unhappy, but we have learned to accept their unhappiness with good grace.

We got in a taxi at Brisbane airport one evening and when we told the driver where we wanted to be taken, an outer suburb, he said no.

"No?!" my friend echoed, but that grin came to his face. "Then we're not going anywhere. And you're not going anywhere." He lounged back on the seat beside me, pulled out a magazine he had bought in the airport and pretended to read; it was actually too dark to read anything.

The poor guy's first decision was to turn off his engine, but he soon came under pressure from the other drivers lined up behind him; a couple blew their horns. He held out for only a couple of minutes.

***

One earlier time, before we had perfected our trick of just jumping in, a taxi pulled up right outside our theatre; the driver shouted his destination question through the open passenger window. When he did not like what he heard from us he took a quick look to check on

102

any traffic and made to pull away, but Rod had stepped in front of the vehicle. There was now a space *behind* the cab and I thought the driver might reverse to give himself more turning room so I jumped in behind it. The team was in action; vehicle could now move neither forward or backward.

However we didn't have a complete victory on that occasion because the driver, a big strong-looking guy, turned off the engine and got out, in what I might call a meaningful way, and with a very meaningful tyre lever in his hand. We decided we preferred the taxi that was at that moment pulling up on the other side of the road.

***

Back to our present journey. Rod and the driver are now engaged in defining just what 'real work' is. The language has become shall we say very informal. Rod never loses the half-smile that comes upon him in these situations, and one time I observe the driver's shoulders shake, from what I suspect is a suppressed laugh in response to one of Rod's more inventive sallies.

All this continues right up to the moment we reach our hotel. I get out---they are still going at it---and fish out the money. I hand the notes in the window and the driver takes them without even looking at them; he has fully turned in his seat to face his tormentor, the first opportunity he has had to do this.

I am owed two dollars but I find myself saying "keep the change"; the driver doesn't acknowledge or possibly even hear what I regard, under the circumstances, is an extremely kind offer.

Rod and driver reach what to them seems to be a satisfactory climax to their 'discussion' and Rod joins me on the footpath. The driver gives a wave as he goes and Rod starts whistling as we walk into the hotel foyer. A good time had by all.

TWELVE

QUEEN OF THE BALL

"Do you get lonely Aunt?"

The two women were sitting on the verandah, the younger woman's husband playing cricket with their boys on the lawn below.

"Why ever do you ask that? Lonely? What a question dear."

"That's a 'no' then is it?"

"Definitely. I've got you and your family---and I've got more on my plate than I sometimes know what to do with. So, lonely? Never."

"I thought that perhaps---with Uncle Gerald gone.....?"

"No, dear. That was hard of course, at first, but it was three years ago. Life goes on. But do I look lonely? Do I act that way?"

"No, and you certainly do keep yourself busy, with all your committees. I just wonder sometimes---well---familiarity? You know what I mean?"

"I do. But I've got you and Jeffrey and the boys for that." She paused for half a minute. "You know dear, I don't think I need much 'familiarity', as you call it, any more. I seem to get along well enough without it." She paused again. "Do I strike you as something of a cold fish? Well, not cold---cool perhaps?"

"Not towards me---and us."

"But.....?"

"You do keep people at a distance. You know that."

"This is getting deep. Your 'Psychology' training is it? Yes, I suppose I do. I think it comes with the territory."

And the 'territory', if Annabelle had to spell it out, was being one of the town's social leaders. Possibly *the* leader---amongst women anyhow; Presidency of the Hospital Ball Committee might alone have settled that question. Then there was the Hospital Board itself, and the Race Club Committee---drafted on unanimously after her husband, who had been its Chair, had died. Then there were all the other charities, of which she was either a board member or the Patron....and then the Advisory Group for the local High School---the school at which she had taught for years, before she had married.

And she knew she was not just a leader but *prominent*---'out there' as a journalist had written once---often photographed at events by the local paper, and approached by it for her views whenever some issue arose; journalists visiting from bigger centres on the coast were often directed to her door. And she believed she always gave value in those interviews too---always had something to contribute; "a woman of substance" one journalist had written of her, which she'd rather liked.

That her wealth added to her status she of course knew, wealth that had come from the wise investments her solicitor husband had made during his life. But she prided herself she would still have had that 'substance' had she had no money at all; intellect and character, she believed, counted for far more.

***

A week later and a phone call from her niece. When she puts down the phone she sighs; if the previous conversation with Christine about loneliness had surprised her, this one has left her vexed. Why didn't her niece recognise the position the girl held---*could* hold? Did she not see the point---the rightness---of joining her table at the Ball? And as for the reason she had just given for not attending---it was beyond belief! If the girl continued to spend her time in these ways, how on earth would she be able to handle the wealth she would eventually inherit from her, and the position that would go with it?

***

The young woman who had prompted the sigh put down the phone and herself sighed; her aunt was a dinosaur. The world in which she lived was passing; it had really only ever existed for privileged people, people like her aunt, and her aunt's mother, Christine's own grandmother.

She loved her aunt---had many reasons for being grateful to her---and she knew she had just disappointed the woman by turning down the invitation. She knew that what would irritate Annabelle for days to come was the reason she had given.

"Surely this woman could find someone else to mind her children?"

"No. That's why I'm doing it."

"Did she ask you?"

"No Aunt, I offered."

"But---didn't you say she's Aboriginal. They seem to let their children run in and out of each other's houses all the time."

"I know what you're saying Aunt but not in this case. She's very caring of her children; you'd approve. They moved only a few months ago and she has no family here. Her husband works at the Zinc."

"Her husband's working!? Must be a white man."

" Now Aunt....."

"My dear, I've had a lot of experience of Aboriginal people in this district. You should hear what the Hospital Board has to deal with sometimes."

"Maybe so---but this is a worthy case and if you knew the woman you would agree." She had half a mind to reprimand her aunt--- again---on her propensity to stereotype people, but let it go. "She's very shy. Gentle."

"Well that's different. But couldn't she wait till her husband comes back in on one of the breaks they have---to go down to the coast?"

"She's not having a holiday Aunt. Confidentially, Doctor Findon says she needs to have a scan done down there. It's not easy to get in, and that's the earliest date the hospital has."

"Oh---can I help out with some money?"

Typical. You are having a tussle with the woman and she says that sort of thing."I love you Aunt---and on Rachel's behalf I'll say yes, thank you."

"But Christine, surely it would be possible to find someone else to look after the children?"

"Well, they're very young and she's very protective---and I've offered to do it. She's very relieved."

***

Annabelle had remained at her phone table; she sighed again. Her niece 'was letting the side down', as Gerald would have said. Not as spectacularly as the girl's mother had done of course---and Christine was a wonderful girl, decent and honest---and of course she loved her. She was hard-working too---if one could call what she did do work.

***

Christine had once said she was elitist. She had bridled at that, but had later thought that if it were true it was no bad thing; the world needed people who had high standards. People knew where you stood, and could respect that. She had later put that point to the girl, but had been met with "yes, but I'm afraid you sometimes think you are above other people." That had stung. Wretched girl.

Did she think she was above others? She had thought about that too, and had a speech prepared if the subject came up again. "Not all people are equal Christine. Surely you would agree that some have more abilities than others---and some use their abilities better. Does that not entitle them to see themselves as somewhat above the pack?"

And, she could add---but wouldn't---it did not mean that such people were not kind and generous. Christine would know she herself gave freely to causes and charities in the town; she would not be so crass as to remind her niece of the support she had given her, ever since Annabelle's own sister had abandoned the girl and gone off with another man. The private schooling and then the up-front university fees themselves had swallowed huge amounts; even Gerald had fussed over that.

***

But she had to put these thoughts aside because now she had to turn her attention to the question of the seating at the Ball---something which she in fact had never had any difficulty with in previous years but which now had become an issue, because this year she was getting 'help' from her new Vice-President, and that woman would be arriving at the house soon to share the results of her efforts; she was not looking forward to the visit.

***

Paula Jones was much younger than she---late thirties would have been Annabelle's guess---and had grown up in the town.

Annabelle knew that she had not even completed the final years at High School but had taken an ordinary job in a dress shop; she had shown financial judgement however in her choice of boyfriend.

Peter Jones had trained as a mechanic, but started a used-car business shortly after the couple married, and then a new-car dealership. That business had grown enormously, as had, obviously, the couple's wealth; they now lived in a very large new house---a mansion really---gave lavish parties---and, it was clear to every woman in the town, Paula Jones spent a fortune on clothes.

In the last few years the woman had also become very active in the social arena, joining one charity committee after another. Very *very* active. As a member of Annabelle's own Hospital Ball Committee she had come forward with suggestions galore at each meeting, and had proved particularly successful at being able to extract substantial financial support for the hospital from her husband's business contacts. Her rise to the Vice-Presidency had been rapid.

But Annabelle did not like the woman. To her mind Paula Jones had virtually *bought* the Vice-Presidency. Social ambition was one thing---Annabelle didn't disapprove of that---so long as it came with qualities of character, but she had to say she had not yet detected any in this woman.

***

When the Committee had first discussed this year's Ball the Jones woman had offered to do anything to help. Annabelle had tried to think of some task which would not bring the two of them into much personal contact, such as the hiring of tables and chairs, but someone had said "Paula---you'd be ideal for doing the seating", and before she could think of a reason not to allocate that to her the die had been cast.

She understood why that person had suggested Paula do the seating; in the minds of many on the Committee the placing of people at the Ball---at which table, and with which others---was very, very important, and Paula Jones, they knew, would do it with mathematical precision.

Annabelle had never met anyone so knowledgeable---so *decided*---about the 'social merits' of each of the town's citizens. It seemed she had everyone ranked, and in addition, knew which people were 'not speaking' to which. Did she spend all day listening to gossip?

The work the woman had had been doing on the seating would no doubt be a help in avoiding some major faux pas, but in fact this was something she herself had never much worried about; if people couldn't come to a ball and enjoy themselves without fussing about who else was on their table......

Everyone wanted to be on her own table of course, the women anyhow; the men, from her experience, couldn't care less. She believed you could throw all the men into a corner of the hall onto a couple of benches and they wouldn't mind; just keep the beer and the food up to them and they'd be happy. No, it was the women who could be the prickly ones, some of them anyhow.

This year's seating policewoman would be arriving soon, and Annabelle knew she was about to learn much more than she wanted to know about the lives of some of her fellow citizens. Though it was still early in the day she had an urge to have a whisky.

***

On the verandah, after the maid had taken the tea things away, the visitor placed a large sheet of paper on the table. It showed the layout of the ballroom as it would be on the night, with tables down both sides of the hall, angling away from the dance floor, and two tables across the top of the room. Annabelle thought of telling Paula that there would now be two vacancies at her own table, but decided not to; there was still a chance, she hoped, that her niece would change her mind, or that the Aboriginal woman would find an alternative carer.

Paula Jones began on the tables at the sides of the hall, starting with the one nearest the President's. She really did not need to know who was on this table---or on any of the tables---but Paula *had* to tell her. The woman said that because this table was nearest the President's, it of course had more prestige, and so she had had to be most careful to get the seating right there; this one had recently been a generous donor, this one was always on that table, this one was good friends with that, and so on.

She listened dutifully, thinking that the woman could not possibly intend to go into such detail on all the other tables---that this would be the only one to receive such treatment. However, by the time they had reached the third, she realised that this was exactly what would happen. She murmured that Paula had certainly done a thoughtful job and that she was quite confident that all the seating had been decided with equal care---you don't need to go on and on woman---but her guest did not take the hint.

She had almost stopped listening when she found herself looking at the two tables at the top end of the hall. *Two* tables, when usually there was just the one, the President's. She interrupted the woman's flow to query it.

"Oh I thought, since there is plenty of space there we might as well use it. We do have heavy bookings."

Annabelle noticed the letters VP placed against one.

"And you thought a Vice-Presidential table would be appropriate?"

"Yes---don't you think?"

"Actually no, Paula. We've always had just the one table there---just the President's."

"I know, but I thought it could be good to make a change. This time."

Yes---a chance for everyone to see you up there, to help you win the crown eventually. Well, I won't assist in that.

112

"I don't think so."

"Really? I asked Barbara and Felicity and they both thought it was a good idea."

Yes they would, with both of them in your little coterie. "No, I don't want any change from how we usually do it. It's worked well in the past. I like the fact that people can feel free to come up to have a chat with the President during the Ball. An extra table could make that difficult."

"Very well," and the woman went on to talk about the seating at the fourth table, but now, Annabelle thought, in a more perfunctory manner. When she had finished with all the tables, she was offered fresh tea, but declined. "Must rush."

***

After her visitor had gone, she remained on the verandah; she needed time to calm down. The nerve of the woman, trying to set up a new table in her own name---and she on the Committee for just two years! Her proposition had had nothing to do with spreading the seating, or making things more 'comfortable'. The only comfort would have been to her, to elevate her position, and to push herself into the spotlight.

Had Paula Jones joined this committee---any of her committees--- just to serve her own social ambitions? Did she care at all about what these groups were trying to achieve? And---yes Christine, I am elitist---the woman was ignorant: ignorant of world affairs, of history, of literature. There was nothing---*nothing*---in the woman's nature or character that she could admire. She had money---well, her husband *made* money, lots of it apparently---but that seemed to be the only 'quality' the woman thought she needed to bring to a cause. Well, she wasn't going to be Queen of this Ball.

***

It had been a shocking thing when her sister had left her husband with her only child, Christine, just ten. And then---what to do with the girl? When she had talked with the deserted father, he seemed to have no ideas. She could see that if left to him the girl would go off in time to the local High School, to possibly leave school early, get some kind of very ordinary job until she got married---early---or, she feared, became a single mother, like so many other girls in the town.

She and Gerald had had no children, but she determined to now give this girl the best of everything. She decided that she should go to a private boarding school, and what better than the one she herself had attended in the capital?

The girl had proved to be a very good student, and it was obvious she was bound for university. Annabelle hoped she would choose Law or Economics, but she had chosen Arts, and, in an early sign of her interests, had majored in Psychology and Sociology. She had just finished her degree when she announced she would return to their town and work in Community Services. And marry Jeffrey, a boy whom she had known since childhood, and who had just finished a mechanics apprenticeship in the town; Annabelle had known a friendship existed, but hadn't imagined it was anything stronger.

These decisions had massively disappointed her. Because the girl was so smart---so good at her studies---she had pictured a stellar career for her, perhaps travelling the world. Instead, she was now going to have a relatively low-paid position in her home town, caring for people who were even more lowly-paid, if employed at all. And married to a *mechanic*.

***

In the ten years that had passed the couple had had two children, and Annabelle had to admit that the marriage was a good one; Jeff was nice, and hard working, their boys a delight, and Christine herself was a happy soul. Though she wondered how the girl managed to be that way, when she heard from her some of the things her job involved---trying to find accommodation for the homeless---resolving domestic disputes---helping illiterate people to fill in claim forms....

***

She had tried to help the couple financially, but the girl had been a reluctant recipient. She wanted Jeff, she said, to feel that he was capable of looking after his own family. She did understand that, but had been allowed to do some things---pay for a holiday on the Reef, and help them get a bigger car.

She called in to see them often, when she drove down the hill from "Farnworth", and had them up at the big old house for weekend barbecues or tennis; in warm weather they used her pool.

Christine was happy to come to informal parties there but was reluctant to attend anything more formal, events that she perversely described as 'Society'; "rich people flaunting their wealth." But didn't the girl appreciate that most of these people were also generous supporters of charities in the town? And---the irony---that she herself was going to be rich one day?

What would she do with that money? Likely give most of it away. Or start some Foundation for deserted wives or abused kids or the likes---which would be better, as long as it did real good, and the funds were well managed. But she did hope they would keep the old house, and move up into it.

***

If there had been changes in her niece's life over the past ten years, there had been changes in her own too. Within herself. She knew that she was less tolerant of people now. More accurately, she would have said---in her own defence---that she was less tolerant of people's inability or unwillingness to face up to reality---or their own shortcomings.

As a result, she found that she didn't so much look forward to being in company anymore. Or was that just what happened when one got older? She thought possibly it was---but then she knew women of her age who still loved company---so perhaps it was just she.

She gave as much to the charities in town as she had always done---more---but she found she no longer had much interest in the details of the work they did, did not in fact really want to *know*, and certainly no longer wanted to be closely involved. Where in earlier days she had taken her turn on stalls and stands, and sold tickets or just 'did things', she was more than happy now to leave all that to others.

Had she been more 'hands-on' when she had come to the town as a young teacher? Yes, she had; she had known the names of all the boys and girls in her classes, and had gladly worked extra hours with any that were having difficulties. She had given up whole weekends to help any that had reading problems; she had got to know many of the parents.

Was this withdrawal now partly due to the superiority thing Christine had accused her of? She didn't think it was---but was it? Were people saying those kinds of thing about her now---even her friends? And---who were her friends now? She realised she had not spent relaxed time with almost anybody for weeks. Months! Christine and Jeff and the boys, that was about it. But did she miss that further contact at all? And if she didn't, was that a worry?

***

Christine had always insisted that whenever she was down in the town she should call in, and she did do that, if she knew that the girl was home and had no other visitors. While Christine had a Department office in the CBD she worked from home a lot of the time. Annabelle had met some of the girl's 'clients' there, accidentally---ones that had called at the house after she had arrived---but she was uncomfortable in their presence. She found them by and large ill-mannered, or perhaps not so much ill-mannered as *lacking* in manners. And---she would not have observed this to anyone, let alone her niece---they were generally so badly *groomed*; just because you did not have much money, you could surely still make an effort. And their children allowed to do anything! Where was the discipline? It was no wonder they were in the position they were in.

Yet Christine *worked* with these people, and, from what she could see, good naturedly and non-judgementally. She had overheard the girl explaining patiently to a woman how to set out a budget, and to another why it was a good idea to have her children vaccinated ---and actually arranging to pick up that woman and her kids to take them to the clinic. Didn't these people have any motivation of their own? Did they really need someone to tell them about the need for vaccinations?

Why, she had once asked her niece, did she did not tell them to come to her office in the centre of town? The girl had said that some of them felt intimidated by the atmosphere of a big organisation in a big building; she said they felt less free to talk about their issues there, even to her. "And some of them---some of the women---are embarrassed Aunt. And they have little kids with them, and they can be hard to control in a place like that." She could certainly believe that.

She always excused herself as soon as she could if someone came to the house; she suffered the introductions and then drove away.

***

One recent Saturday when she was at Christine's they had chatted a while then Christine excused herself, saying she had one little work detail she needed to finalise; Annabelle could hear her using the phone in her back office, though not what she was saying. Christine rejoined her but fifteen minutes later there was knock at the front door and Christine admitted a young woman with four small children. She rose to leave but Christine waved her back into her chair---rather authoritatively she thought.

"Stay Aunt. This won't take long. You don't have to dash off." She had sat, and so had been introduced to Lorraine and her children, aged she would have thought between two and six. The woman was a 'client' of Christine's---an odd term she always thought, but just part of the 'management speak' all the Government departments now seemed to employ.

The visitor had not been able to make head nor tail of some Centrelink forms Chistine had left with her. Surprising herself, Annabelle asked if she could help, and when the woman agreed, began going over the papers. Her next surprise came when she read that Lorraine, who had already filled in the identity section of the forms, was only twenty-four.

She had struggled to find common ground in conversation with the visitor but eventually did, and in, of all things, literacy; the woman said she was determined that her children would be good readers and writers, and so even though she had difficulties there herself, she would be making sure they went to the library often and borrowed books. She said she knew it was important to read to children---though she said her mother had never done that with her. Annabelle made a mental note to ask Christine to buy a quantity of suitable books for the family, for which she would pay.

She stayed at Christine's after the woman and her children had left. Her niece was looking at her with a smile on her face.

"Yes I know. What did you say---'familiarity'? How did I do?

"Wonderfully. What next I wonder?"

"I wonder too---about Lorraine. I was looking at her handwriting. It was laboured."

"Yes. Not uncommon."

"Does she have a husband?"

"Partner."

That would be right. "And is he working?"

"Was. Got put off at the Zinc when they closed. It's just for maintenance they said, and he'll start again soon."

"That's something. But---all those children---and she's so young. At least she's not pregnant again, not to my eyes anyhow."

"You can thank me for that."

She stared; the girl laughed. "The look on your face!"

"Well---what do you mean?"

"They taught us that people of lower socio-economic groups are often the more conservative people in society. There's a case. She couldn't talk to her doctor about contraception."

"But---the pill? It's been around for donkey's years."

"Maybe so---but there you are."

"So what did you....?"

"I told her I took it, and showed her the packet. I actually gave her one. Shouldn't have---they have to be prescribed. Then I made an appointment with a doctor; I actually went along with her."

***

That night while she was watching television her mind tracked back to the girl with four children. Would she be able to read to them from the books she would get? It might need to be done by someone else---perhaps someone from the library. She would speak to Christine the next day.

Her phone rang. "Hello Annabelle. It's Paula. I'm just calling about those tables again. I'm wondering if you have thought any more about a Vice-Presidential table?"

"No I haven't Paula. My mind is made up on that."

"Well it's just that another Committee member has told me she thinks it could be a good idea......"

"Did she? Who?"

The woman named one of the younger members of the Committee, a girl really---on trainer wheels in her opinion---and someone who always seemed to back any proposition that Paula Jones put up.

Anger welled up within her. Impudent, pushy woman. Did she think I can't see that this is all just a cloak for her social ambitions?! She allowed a silence to extend; let her stew.

"Well Paula, we live in a democracy. We've got this meeting of the full committee next week. Since we disagree on the point, why don't you bring it up there." And won't you be busy now rounding up the numbers.

***

The Committee meetings were held in the same big room at the hospital that the Board used; Annabelle arrived a quarter of an hour early, but everybody was there already. She settled herself in her place at the head of the table and began to look through the Minutes Book and some of her notes. It seemed to her there was a heightened atmosphere in the room---a buzz; she wondered if Paula's proposal was the cause.

They caught each other's eyes and the younger woman gave a little wave; she smiled in return---but really she could not take to this one. And she had acknowledged to herself that part of the reason was rather a petty one: the way the younger woman had first began addressing her. She was a full generation older, so at first it should have been "Mrs. Chambers", but the younger woman had used her Christian name from the very beginning, and in, she thought, an overly familiar manner; it had irked her.

Paula seemed to be very animated as she talked with some of the others, and had she gone to greater lengths with her appearance? Her make-up seemed to be fuller, her hair was done in an elaborate coif, and the dress---was it silk? A lot of effort had been put in; was all that to help her case?

***

As soon as she and the Secretary had dealt with the usual 'housekeeping' she raised the matter of the extra table and invited Paula to speak to it. The woman did this well, Annabelle thought, if perhaps a little nervously.

She asked Paula to put the idea as a motion so that they could have a formal debate on it and then proceed to a vote. The woman said that she had hoped it wouldn't come to a motion, that they might just agree or disagree to it. Annabelle said that from her long experience she had learned it was better to have matters put to a vote; it was then in the Minutes and precluded any questions later on. Paula put the motion and one of her 'friends' seconded it.

When Annabelle asked if anyone wanted to speak against it there was silence---as if everyone had already made up their minds. Did they, she wondered, see this as a power struggle between us two? She filled the silence after a moment by putting her own views--- why it worked better as it was. When she had had her say she again invited others to speak. One spoke for Paula's idea and one against but only briefly. She then called for a show of hands--- and Paula's proposition was voted down comprehensively. Annabelle then called for 'other business'.

***

Coffee was served at the end of the meeting and people then began drifting off. She was gathering up her notes when Paula approached.

"Well Annabelle, you got your way on that one." Quite hostile.

"I don't look at it in that way. We put the idea and it was defeated. End of story. Perhaps if it comes up again in the future it will succeed."

"Not while you are President."

Annabelle was shocked by the words, but even more by the tone! She had been continuing to put papers into her folder but now she looked sharply at the other woman. She saw that her face had a pinched look---drawn almost; this had meant a lot to her.

"You have a lot to learn about being a committee member young lady."

"Well, Annabelle...." but she cut her off with "and a word on the subject of my name. It is Mrs. Chambers to you---until I say otherwise. Good morning."

***

The books she had ordered for Lorraine arrived on a Friday and the next day she phoned Christine.

"Oh good, Aunt. They'll be thrilled to get them. Could you possibly bring them down now?

"Yes."

"I'd take them round to Lorraine myself but Jeff's taken the boys fishing in the station waggon and I've lent the Corolla to a friend for the morning. Could you take them to her?"

She found the street, one which she had never been in before; she had in fact never been in that part of town. As she drove along she was aware of incongruity---a long, large Mercedes gliding past tiny old timber cottages.

***

She was taken into the central room of the house, a combined dining, lounge and rumpus room, and she put the two packages of books on the table.

"Do you mind if I open them?" Lorraine asked.

"No---do."

The children climbing onto chairs were told by their young mother not to touch any of the books until she said so. When they were all out---and there were more than twenty---she looked at Annabelle with tears in her eyes.

"It's like Christmas! Thank you, thank you so much. We'll look after them, won't we kids." The little ones nodded solemnly, but hands were inching forward.

"Those are picture books for the littlee's but these will be good reading ones---about growing up in the country."

After she left she felt so buoyed she drove back to her niece's; she noticed that Chistine's Corolla was now in the driveway.

"I felt like Santa Claus. The reading books are a bit beyond the two older ones now but that's good. When Lorraine reads to them that will help them want to learn to read." She stopped. "*Will* she be able to read to them?"

"Probably not. Don't you remember those forms she couldn't manage? She is barely literate."

"Well her partner then?"

"Not that one I'm afraid."

"Well, someone---a family friend?"

Christine looked doubtful. "We'll see. What we need in this town is people who like reading and who have spare time---or who will *make* the time."

That evening she rang her niece to say *she'd* be happy to read to Lorraine's children. The girl accepted the offer without expressing any surprise, almost, Annabelle thought, as if she were expecting it.

***

Later that night Millie Secombe the Ball Committee Secretary rang to say that Paula Jones was resigning from the Committee, citing ill health. As Annabelle lay in bed before going to sleep she thought that all in all it had been a good week.

***

Lorraine rang her the next day to say that Christine had told her of her offer and of course she accepted. But when would be the best time? The two littlees could be read to anytime during the day, but for the two school aged ones their bed-time was best; Annabelle agreed to come that evening.

She arrived at seven-thirty to find all the children bathed and in their pyjamas. She met Dwayne, who was polite but seemed, she thought, a little uncomfortable. He excused himself and went back to the television program he had been watching and she went to the children's bedroom.

In that small house all four children slept in the one room, an enclosed verandah. Lorraine had already placed a lounge chair between the beds of the five and six year olds, with a lamp behind it.

Annabelle decided to read from "The Bush Bunnies" series; the two children lay back, staring at the ceiling, and seeming to hang on every word. Sometimes one or the other would interrupt to ask a question, or to 'contribute'. Whenever she came to an illustration she tried showing it to first one then the other, but both wanted to look at the same moment, and leaned out of their beds onto her. They felt so warm---and smelled, she thought, so nice.

What she hadn't thought would happen was that the two younger ones also paid close attention, from their own beds. After a while they left them and came up to stand beside her. Eventually the youngest crawled into her lap, and the other sat on her feet, her arms around her legs.

Lorraine came to the door and went away again, to return with her husband. Annabelle looked at the two smiling faces in the doorway with what she was sure must have been a silly grin on her own face. How's this for familiarity Chris?

***

Millie the secretary rang again the next day to say that she had gone to see Paula Jones to collect the seating plan. She said that she thought the woman did not look well, and had heard that she was retiring from other committees too. It seemed as if her 'public life' was coming to an end, at least for now.

***

She read again to the children two evenings later. This time she shared a cup of coffee with the couple afterwards. She thought Lorraine was a happy and positive girl despite circumstances that she herself would have found difficult. Dwayne did not say much, but neither did he withdraw to watch television. She managed to get him to tell her about the job he hoped to return to shortly. As she drove home that evening she thought she might make the offer to help the girl with her own reading.

She felt happy, and she wondered at that. If she had been asked to explain, she might have said it was as if she had just discovered new members of her own family. Nice ones.

***

She called at Christine's office in the town centre to share her pleasure over what had occurred the night before. She learned that Lorraine had already phoned her niece to say how much the children were enjoying the visits.

The phone on the desk buzzed and Christine told the receptionist to send the client in. Annabelle rose to go, but Christine motioned her to stay. When she put the phone down she said it was the Aboriginal woman whose children she was going to mind on the night of the Ball; there were some forms the woman needed to fill in for the coast hospital; she would like Annabelle to meet Rachel.

A tall slim woman entered, with three small children. Annabelle realised she had never seen or noticed the woman in the streets. While Christine showed her which parts of the forms she needed to fill in, marking them with pencil, the woman occasionally looked across at Annabelle.

The children were well dressed and quiet. Annabelle asked about them and Rachel told her the eldest one was doing very well at school. The little family stayed for only a few minutes.

***

"She seems nice."

"She's lovely. Very shy. She comes from a little town up north; this place is a metropolis to her. I do hope this thing isn't anything too serious---but Doctor Findon suspects a tumour. In the stomach. It would mean an operation of course."

"I said I'd like to help. Can I give you some money for them?"

"Yes you can Aunt, thank you. And the quicker the better. If she has to go back down there for an operation they are going to have a lot of extra expenses. 'Health' will cover a good deal, but there are always extra things. If you could give me a small cheque now I can put it into our 'Donations' account and then I'll pass it on to her. I never say these things are donations---I hide that." Annabelle wrote out a cheque for two hundred dollars and passed it across. "Thank you Aunt, but you'd better not come here too often; we'll make you poor."

***

It was now just three weeks to the ball. All the committee women had their duties and were getting on with them but one or other of them still rang her each day about something. Millie said that another committee member who had just visited Paula Jones told her that the woman was indeed unwell; Millie had taken it onto herself to send flowers and a 'get well' card.

***

Annabelle had earlier mentioned to Christine the Paula Jones tables issue, and now she told her about the scene at the hospital after the Committee meeting.

"Wow. You told her to address you in future as Mrs. Chambers?"

"Yes. The woman lacks respect for others. It will do her good. Although I may have put some sort of curse on her; I hear she has become unwell."

A day later Christine told her that she too had heard that the woman was really ill.

"I know you don't like her Aunt, but what if she has some serious condition? Could you bring yourself to visit her and see for yourself---maybe mend some fences?"

Typical of Saint Christine to say something like that---and she was not at all inclined---but then she heard from another of the Hospital Ball committee members who had seen the Jones woman in the front garden of her house and thought she had lost weight. 'Look what you've got me doing now Christine'; she rang the woman's number.

127

The phone was answered by a nurse, who told her Paula was resting; she asked the nurse to inquire if she might drop in. The nurse was gone for such a long time that Annabelle was sure that the answer would be no, but it was Paula herself who came on the line. "I look a sight---but please come. It's nice of you."

***

All life seemed to have been drained from the woman's face. Her eyes were sunken, and seemed to burn. "Would you like some tea Mrs.Chambers. Janice can make some." Her voice too was different.

"Oh please, call me Annabelle," embarrassed now by her remarks of a fortnight before. "No, no tea thank you. But whatever is it Paula?"

The woman touched her chest. "These. I had a double mastectomy and chemotherapy five years ago, but they said it could come back. Nothing to do about it this time I'm afraid."

"Oh my dear....."

"The luck of the draw. My mother had it. And I left it too late."

The woman's composure broke, and she dropped her head and began to cry. Annabelle moved her chair closer and took her hands. "I should say 'if there is anything I can do', but of course I know there is nothing---of real value."

They stayed together like that for minutes, and then the woman shook herself and wiped her eyes. "I will have some good days the doctors tell me. Remission; that can even last for weeks." She smiled. "Actually I've been feeling not too bad these last few days. Perhaps I'll get to the Ball after all; I spent enough on the dress!"

In the days that followed Annabelle took to visiting Paula Jones every afternoon, Annabelle talking about her life and Paula about hers. The thrusting, judgemental and socially ambitious Paula disappeared, replaced by a calmer and more generous-hearted one. Annabelle came to the conclusion that the aggressiveness of Paula's social ambitions had sprung from this illness---a need to claim as many of what she saw as life's prizes as she could before it was too late, the vice presidential table at the head of the hall being one of them.

Paula obviously enjoyed her visits, and they coincided with a marked improvement in her appearance. She regained some weight, and during one visit the woman even modelled her ball gown. She was in remission.

***

Christine remained adamant that she would not be attending the Ball---that she would be looking after Rachel's children as she had promised. Annabelle moved another couple up onto her table.

***

Four days before the Ball her niece rang. "You'd better not come to the house till I say. I'm coming down with something; you shouldn't risk catching it at the moment, not just before your big 'do'. I'm aching all over today; I feel as if I've been run over by a truck."

When Annabelle rang the girl the next day she learned that their mutual doctor had diagnosed flu; she had been ordered into isolation, and to rest.

"Oh. What are we going to do about Rachel?"

"I know. I've been trying to think of someone to help out but I haven't yet. And she'll cancel her trip for the scan if it's not me---or someone else she knows and trusts---and she says she doesn't know anyone. I'm thinking.

By the way, I have to get those forms back from her but obviously I shouldn't go near her at the moment. Could you possible pick them up for me, and then drop them in my letterbox?" She gave Annabelle the address.

When she called at the house the woman, very tentatively, asked her if she wouldn't mind looking at the forms to see if she had filled them in properly; they did this together at the kitchen table. Rachel offered to make tea and while she did, one of the little ones came up with a book, and she put the girl onto her lap to read to her. After a while one of the other children joined them, and she read to them for over an hour; I could have a new full time job, she thought.

Rachel knew Christine had flu, but neither woman mentioned that she would then be unavailable to mind the children. I could offer, she thought, if it weren't for the Ball. Back at her own house she did more thinking about it.

"Have you been able to do anything about Rachel yet?"

"No. I don't know what to tell her."

"Would Rachel be happy with me minding her children?"

"You?! I'd say so. She's rung me to say how helpful you were. She thinks you're nice. But Aunt....?"

"I know, I know---but that woman has to have that scan done straight away." She took a breath. "Make the offer darling." Within an hour Christine had rung back to say that Rachel had accepted; Annabelle went straight to see Paula Jones.

***

At ten o'clock on the night of the ball, with the three children now asleep, Annabelle walked out onto the little porch. The cottage was well away from the town's centre, but the sound of the orchestra carried up to her on the cold, still air. She shivered, and wrapped her arms around herself, but stayed where she was.

She wondered if the Ball were living up to the standard of past ones, but then she thought, why wouldn't it; it had after all been organised by an expert. And really, all that was not so hard---if one did the planning---and had standards.

She hoped that Paula Jones was enjoying it---Queen of the Ball after all; one could not begrudge that woman any nice thing now. And she realised that she herself felt perfectly content, with where she was and what she was doing. Although she wished she knew what a manipulating niece had in mind for her next.....

THIRTEEN

THE DISAPPEARANCE OF CHRISTINE HOLMES

– PART 1 –

"If you like mysteries so much, why don't you look at the Christine Holmes case?" This from the editor at the North Queensland newspaper I had joined as a reporter six months before; I had shown an interest in unsolved crimes of the area.

"It was during the War. It's a beauty. No-one ever found the woman---dead or alive. Just after I came here I dug out all the stuff the paper did on it. There's quite a lot; people kept banging on about it for years."

***

"WOMAN MISSING---FEARS HELD" was the headline in the edition of Wednesday September 20th 1944. "Police are seeking the public's help in finding missing woman Christine Holmes. The woman, aged thirty-eight, disappeared from Farley Station last weekend, while her family and station staff were at the Parker River rodeo.

The woman's husband, well known Cape York cattleman Roger Holmes, has told police his wife was well when he and their children and the ringers left Farley last Thursday morning. Mr. Holmes said it was not unusual for his wife to stay behind at the homestead, on her own, when the family went off to rodeos.

A thorough search is still being made of the bushland surrounding Farley Station homestead and police divers are also dragging lagoons in the nearby Lake River.

Police Sergeant Connell said that grave fears are held for Mrs. Holmes' welfare. At the moment the police have no clues as to the woman's whereabouts, and are asking the public to contact them if they have any information. The accompanying photograph of Mrs. Holmes is a recent one and is said to be a good likeness."

The photo was a head and shoulders shot of an attractive woman with medium length brown or black hair. The caption under the photo said it had been taken by her daughter only two months before, during a visit by the two of them to a US air force base, which was not far from Farley. The woman looked, I thought, younger than her thirty-eight years.

Each subsequent edition of our paper carried the story, on page one then page two and then page three and so on; it gradually slipped further back, as no further developments were reported. The last report appeared three months later, in late December; it was brief, saying simply that police had no new information about the woman's whereabouts and were still asking for the public's assistance.

"You'll find a few more articles later on, if you're interested" Jim told me. "Feature stuff. Nothing new in them---just returning to the story. There's one by a woman called Dulcie Wettenhall you should look at though. It's the best---very thorough."

I found and read Wettenhall's article; the woman had obviously done more research than the earlier writers. I learned that the missing woman was born Christine Mendoza, in 1906, into a large family of Spanish descent. She had left school at fifteen to work in a produce store on the edge of town here, serving behind the counter and sometimes helping in the office. Women who had also worked there at that time told the writer that she had been a good worker; they also said she was very pretty and always dressed well, and was very much a favourite with people who came into the store.

Roger Holmes first met her at that store; they married in 1927, when she was twenty-one and he twenty-eight, and moved to Farley. The young couple set up home in a cottage near the main homestead. A boy was born the following year, followed by a girl two years later, another girl a year after that and another boy two years later still. When Roger Holmes' parents retired into town here, they moved across into the homestead.

When Christine disappeared the eldest child was sixteen, the youngest eleven. Five years after the disappearance, Roger Holmes moved himself and his family to town, putting a manager on at Farley. When Dulcie wrote this follow-up---in 1965---two of the offspring had moved down south; when she contacted the two who had remained in town she said that neither had had anything new to add to what had already been reported and written about many times.

Though the father declined to be interviewed again, he did give permission for the writer to visit the property. There she met the incumbent manager and his wife, and took photos of the homestead; it looked typical of homesteads I have seen throughout this part of Australia---single storeyed and quite wide, on stumps about two metres high, a steeply pitched roof and a verandah across the front and down both sides.

She also took a photo from the front verandah looking at the front garden. It seemed to be mainly lawn, with what looked like a frangipanni near the front steps, some bougainvilleas trained across mesh giving shade to part of the front path, and a tree that I took to be a mango, about five metres tall, just inside the front gate. The front fence seemed to be of mesh, a metre or so high; one could clearly see the road just the other side of the gate.

Wettenhall met some of the people on stations round about who had known Christine. She wrote that they all spoke well of her: friendly, funny---a good neighbour---"the life of any party". One said that although Christine had fitted in well to their 'community'---and seemed to be a good mother---she stood out. "She could look glamorous at the drop of a hat---put the rest of us to shame," one woman said. None had any considered opinions as to what had happened to her; it seemed to be as much of a mystery to them as to the police.

***

"We came home from the rodeo and our mother was gone. That was all." Dorothy, Christine's elder daughter, now eighty-three, was sharing a cup of coffee with me in her house.

"What did you think, you and your brothers and sister? And your father?"

"Well, we didn't know what to think. But it was awful---for days and weeks afterwards. I was only sixteen. I think I missed her the most. Mum was a young sort of person---more like a sister to me in a way. Mum and me and my younger sister used to have 'dress-ups' sometimes, and she'd let us put on her clothes and make-up. She had wigs too; when she put them on you'd hardly recognise her. When she dressed up for a party she looked really beautiful. Everyone was always happy to see Mum.

You know, we had a really good social life up there. People get bush life wrong. I used to tell them down here we had more real contact with people there than you have here in town. There was the two-way radio for one thing---we were always speaking to someone

136

on that. And we'd go to 'Wonga' or 'Beersheeba' for tennis---stay overnight of course. And we'd have dances; just some boards put down on a lawn, and records, but they were great. We were lucky too because the road to the Top went right past our house, so there were always people calling in. And then there were the Americans, at their air force base. That was only forty miles away over near the coast, and they used to put things on out there. They even let us climb into the planes."

"I am trying to imagine what it would have been like for me if my mother had vanished."

"It was like Mum had just gone to town---to the hospital or something, like when she had my youngest brother. I think we all thought she'd just turn up. Only---eventually of course....."

"I know it's not nice to imagine, but do you think she was killed by someone?"

"I have thought that---sometimes---but then the thought just goes out of my head. It's not something you want to think about. You can't really. And anyhow, why would someone do that?"

"Well, there are crazies..."

She nodded. "Yes, I know. I think we just pushed all that to the back of our minds." As one probably would, I thought.

"Can you remember how your father was? Did he get depressed?"

"No, he seemed to just go on with life---the way we all did. I remember him getting angry a lot though."

"Angry?"

"Yes, whenever we brought it up. Seemed to get angry with *us*. I suppose that wasn't the case, but...."

"Angry at what the disappearance had done to his life? To *your* lives?"

"I suppose. I think she must have been abducted really. What else could have happened? She wouldn't have just gone away and left us. Her kids. And Dad."

She said that some Aboriginals who lived in a little settlement further down the river had come up to try to help, looking for tracks. The homestead was surrounded by red dirt, and they found many tracks that belonged to Christine, but they only led to and from the clothesline or the henhouse. There was one clear and recent track showing she had walked to the nearby lagoon, but also one showing she had returned. They said there was no sign of any "strange" footprints around the homestead. There were many signs of vehicles on the road, but then it was busy in the Dry. Since the U.S. air force base had been set up nearby two years earlier, the traffic had apparently grown much heavier.

***

Dulcie Wettenhall's feature article pointed out that no note had been left by the woman; this had led to a widely held theory that the woman had been kidnapped. But by whom, and why---and had she been taken north or south? The writer concluded in 1965 that since no-one had brought forward any new evidence in twenty-one years, the disappearance was likely to remain a mystery.

***

I found out that Roger Holmes died in 1986 and only two of the couple's four children were now still alive, the woman I had interviewed and her younger brother, who was eighty and had dementia. She had told me which nursing home he was in and I visited him, but his mental condition was such that he could add nothing useful. He did remember climbing over some big trucks, which I think may have been at the American base.

***

Did I have some idea I might be able to solve this mystery? Not realistically I suppose---but there was that lingering thought. I decided to drive to the station homestead---'visit the scene of the crime', as all good detectives do. It was only some two hundred kilometres up the Cape on what I was told was a good road and I reasoned I could drive there and back in the day. I asked the daughter Dorothy if she would like to come with me and she said yes. I rang the current owners of Farley, half expecting that they might not be agreeable to a visit, but they were, and when the old woman and I arrived we were made very welcome, and given carte blanche to look wherever we wanted, even throughout the house itself.

I do not know what I expected to find. Of course there were no traces of Christine Holmes and her family in the house; the disappearance had occurred seventy years before, and her husband and their children had continued to live in the house for only five years more before moving to town.

Dorothy asked if she could go into the bedroom she had shared with her sister. She seemed to want to linger there so I went outside and wandered around the garden. I tried to put myself in Christine's place. Had she been outside when a car or vehicle had pulled up? Had she walked over to the front gate and there been overcome and put in the vehicle? Standing there myself in that peaceful bright sunshine I could scarcely credit it.

And who could have done it? Someone she knew? Or an itinerant, seizing an opportunity? To rape? To murder? But if this did happen, where was her body? Police reported that they searched an extensive area around the homestead, and the roadsides for kilometres north and south. But if the abductor had driven a long way, and then down some side track, finding her final resting place would have been like looking for the proverbial needle. Cape York was very sparsely populated at that time, as it still is.

Of course I had admitted to myself that the woman might simply have absconded, but since no vehicle was missing from the station that would have meant there must have been an accomplice. That line would surely have been followed by the police, in their many interviews of the locals, but it seemed nothing useful had emerged. And then, supposing there had been a co-conspirator amongst them---someone who had stayed in the area after the disappearance ---wouldn't he or she have let slip something over the years? Or wouldn't a friend or acquaintance or a relative have had suspicions, then or later, and said something to someone?

And what might any accomplice have done? Picked Christine up and driven her to, say, our town? Would Christine have then caught a train south?

If that had happened, did the woman then try to begin a new life somewhere? That sort of thing happens; one only has to look at the "Missing Persons" board in the foyer of any Police Station. I suppose she could have given herself a new name, and invented a 'story' for her life up to then. And if she had steered clear of any 'Authority' she might never have had to produce a birth certificate and such like.

The woman was attractive and popular---with women and men--- "the life of the party". Could she have formed a relationship with a man in her region, a station owner or manager, or even a stockman? Or a man who visited the station regularly, such as a mailman, or a linesman, or a tradesman?

But this woman was surrounded by family; surely someone would have noticed a growing attachment. The children might have been too young to recognise the signs I suppose, and it was possible the woman had been so careful that even her husband had not suspected. Some of the comments attributable to him in the articles I read had led me to think that Roger Holmes was not very thoughtful or curious about human behaviour. He may not have been good at managing staff either; one of the neighbours said in the police interviews that it was hard to keep track of the employees on Farley because the owner kept firing them.

I remembered there was a tone in Dulcie Wettenhall's article which I thought showed a certain 'attitude' towards the man. Had she concluded that the marriage was not a happy one, and that Christine had been discontented with her lot? That anger that his daughter said he exhibited---could that have been because he believed that his wife *had* run away?

***

On the long drive back to town Dorothy alternately dozed and related memories that the passing countryside brought back to her. After I had dropped her off at her house and was back in my own digs, I thought that though I had learned nothing new by visiting the woman's home, I was glad I had made the journey; I had been where Christine had walked and lived. The place looked very much as I imagine it was seventy years before, the mango tree near the front gate though now huge. Guarding Farley's secret.

FOURTEEN

THE DISAPPEARANCE OF CHRISTINE HOLMES

– PART 2 –

The editor ran my long feature in a weekend edition of the paper: "Cape York's Greatest Mystery---The Disappearance of Christine Holmes in 1944". I had expected that we would get some correspondence on the subject and we did, but what I had not expected was a phone call from the writer of that excellent 1965 article, Dulcie Wettenhall; I think I had assumed she was dead.

***

Waiting for me on a cane lounge on her verandah was an old and frail looking woman, but her eyes were bright and her handshake firm.

"Well young man, what did you learn from that visit to Farley?"

"That I do not know any more than when I read all those articles. Yours was the best."

She nodded, accepting the compliment." But there are things I learned after writing that."

"Do you know what happened to her!?"

"I think I do. She went away voluntarily."

"On her own?"

"No, with a man."

"But the police ruled that out. No-one left the district at that time. They looked at that angle."

She shook her head. "They looked only at the Australian angle."

"An American!?"

"I think so. In fact I think I may know which one."

***

She told me that after she finished her feature for our paper in the early Sixties, she had put the whole question aside, but in the Seventies she was assigned to cover a Defence ceremony at the local airport---the unveiling of a monument to the co-operation between Australian and American air services during the Second World War. Amongst the dignitaries were to be a couple of retired U.S. airmen who had served in this area, and she arranged to interview them; she thought their memories of that time could make good copy.

One of the men had been stationed at the air base near Farley at the time of Christine Holmes' disappearance. He had memory of the event, and could actually recall the woman herself.

He said that Christine was very pretty, and that he used to see her quite often when she drove out to the Base with things that the mailman had left for them at her homestead. The base did have its own mail plane but sometimes other things would come up from town on the regular civilian mail truck. They would be dropped off at the homestead, and the owner or his wife would bring them out to the base in a station vehicle, for which they were paid.

He said that at first it was mostly the man that came out, but towards the end---before she vanished---it was always the woman.

"For the first time after I had written that article, I began to connect some dots. Holmes said that his wife had often chosen to stop at home in that last year, when the rest of the family and even the staff went to rodeos or sports events and the like. Even, eventually, when they all went to town.

Now that I found strange. Not the rodeo bit so much but the town thing. Women up on those stations generally loved a chance to get away to town. Life could be pretty basic up there. Remember, we're talking the 1940's: no air conditioning---probably no freezer---a generator you only started up when power was absolutely needed. Family and often stockmen to cook for. Long working days.

Women up on the Cape tended to take any opportunity to come in here, and I think Christine especially would have loved that; I'd say that there was still a lot of the 'urban' woman in Christine Holmes. She loved meeting people; she was a 'mixer'. And she liked to dress up and look pretty. I reckon she should have relished those trips to town. But her husband said that for a year or so before she disappeared, when the family went to town, she stayed at home---alone.

I remembered something else; one of their boys had told me that sometimes a truck would be driven over from the airbase to pick up anything really bulky that had been dropped off at the homestead. He remembered it was always the same American, a big friendly man he said, with stripes on his sleeves."

"Did you find out his name?"

"No."

"But you think......"

"They could have been having an affair."

"But when or where would they have.....?"

"Got together? Well---those times when everyone went off and she was left on her own; she could easily have got a message to him. Or---over at the airbase? She went over there quite frequently, and if the man was clever he would have arranged some private place."

"So you think they might have run off together. But---an American airman---going awol in Australia---with an Australian married woman!? Wouldn't a pair like that have been picked up?"

"He mightn't have gone awol. What if he was just about to be flown back to the States? This was happening a lot then. There was still some fighting going on in New Guinea in 1944 but really the front line had shifted a long way north, and there wasn't the need for all the American bases here. American forces in Australia were being shipped or flown out all the time, to the new bases in Asia, or home.

Before he left Australia, the man might even have married Christine. From what I've read there were plenty of rushed marriages at that time. She mighn't have been able to provide the right paperwork, but would that have mattered---at that time?"

"Where could that have happened?"

"Well, American ships were going out of Australian ports all the time. It could have been Townsville or Brisbane. Either place. The couple could have easily got down there by train."

"Pretty daring. What if someone had recognised her? There were photos in the paper."

"The wigs, remember? And she could have used different make-up. She could have made herself look older, come to that. No, I think the risks of her being recognised were small. If they had got married she wouldn't have been allowed to go with her new husband on a troopship, but she would only have had to stay in Australia a year or so; we had the Japs pretty much on the run by then remember."

It was of course all supposition, though plausible I thought, at least as plausible as anything else I had read. I decided to do some more digging; would there be a record of American forces personnel in Australia at that time? I found out that there was, and even a list of the men who were at that air base, and detailing their arrival and departure dates.

I checked each entry, a long job, as there were more than four hundred men stationed there, off and on. I found that a Sergeant Rimmington, aged forty, left the base on the very day Christine Holmes was thought to have disappeared. In addition, there was a note beside that entry that he would be delivering a transport lorry back here to town---a drive that would have taken him right past the Farley homestead.

Excited, I rang Dulcie and told her all this. "Come and see me" she ordered. I had been offered a whisky on my earlier visit so after my shift at the paper I picked up a bottle on the way to her house.

***

Hercule proposed a toast, but when we lowered our glasses again Agatha brought us back to earth.

"Of course we both know we haven't proved a thing."

"You're spoiling the moment."

"Well---she could have been abducted. Killed and buried in the bush somewhere."

"By whom?"

"Someone driving past---seeing her in the front garden. The police might not have identified everyone using the road at that time."

"Or.....?"

"Or---someone passing could have given her a lift to town here, and she could have taken the train south."

"But Dulcie," I said, "that person would surely have come forward. There was such a lot of publicity."

"Up *here*. If that person himself was heading south on the train, he would have missed all that. Remember, he could have picked her up as early as the Saturday, and she was only reported missing the following Tuesday, after the family returned from that rodeo; the public would only have heard about it on the Wednesday morning really. So that's four days later."

"But wouldn't it have been reported down in Brisbane too, in the Courier Mail?"

"Well, this was wartime; someone missing from a cattle station on Cape York would not have been big news down there."

"Okay---but then?"

"Well, if she stayed in Brisbane she could have just melted into the population---the way missing persons do today. But she could have gone on to Sydney. Or Melbourne. Anywhere."

We were silent a moment. "I did get pretty excited there about the American airman," I said," but now I'm thinking more--- abduction."

"Didn't run off?"

"Dulcie, she had four young children. Would she have just left them?"

She shrugged. "It happens. Women do run away from situations."

"You mean Roger?"

She nodded. "I didn't actually meet him---just talked to him on the phone. But from that---and some of the things I'd read in those early reports---I don't think I would like to have been married to him. A hard man I thought."

***

We knew we had just been speculating, just as tens and possibly hundreds of people had done over the years. We sipped our whiskies, and allowed our minds to wander off onto other subjects. From that high verandah we watched children playing in the street, riding scooters and bikes, calling out to each other, and laughing. As dusk fell, and lights came on in nearby houses, mothers began calling their offspring inside. They were, I thought, lovely sounds--- sounds the children at Farley would have known well---sounds that ceased in September 1944.

FIFTEEN

THE BEST DAY

Claire woke earlier than usual, and with a feeling of unease. Within a minute the reason for that feeling came back to her; it was going to be the worst day. She groaned, quietly, so as not to wake Don, rolled out of bed, put on t-shirt and shorts, and went out to their kitchen.

She wouldn't think about what lay ahead straight away; she put on coffee, washed her face and combed her hair, and did some stretching exercises. After she poured the coffee she went out onto the deck. Their two butcher birds landed on the railing immediately; did they sit up in those gum trees just waiting for me to appear? She went back to the kitchen to fetch the mince, and, while she was there, some seed.

While the butcher birds and now the lorikeets fed, she allowed herself to contemplate the miseries ahead: the tutorial, the Dean's 'rally', and the Vice-Chancellor's soiree.

At least with the tutorial she would be in charge, but Lord, why did it have to be such hard going? Not the preparation, which was all done and had actually been stimulating, but the response. She understood that only some Australians might be interested in early European History, and that it *was* a step to see the relevance of political and religious and social events of so long ago and so far away to life in Australia today, but the subject was an important part of a course that these undergrads had *chosen*.

She knew that the younger ones might have a struggle to 'get' it, but even the older ones seemed indifferent. Why did so few of them bother to read the extra material she recommended during her lectures? Their contributions during subsequent tutorials as a result were minimal; interesting *questions* would have been something. It was as if they were all just filling in time. When she remembered some of the lively tutorials she had attended as a student..........

"Why are you doing tutorials anyhow?" Don had asked. "You're a professor now."

"Associate, darling. A very new one. And I had these tutorials programmed in before I was 'elevated', and Carmichael asked me to go ahead with them."

"The bastard. You should have said no."

And she should have. She didn't mind doing favours for some people, but that man.....

***

Three quarters of an hour had passed and Don had not yet appeared. She went back to the bedroom.

"I'm awake. Just thought I'd lie here for a bit. I think I'm getting something."

"A cold?"

"Feels like it. I'll get up soon and take something. I don't have to be in the office till ten."

"I don't want to sound heartless and unfeeling darling, but do you think you'll be able to make the Vice Chancellor's do---six o'clock?" His presence would make it bearable.

152

"I'll make it. Dope myself up if I have to. And you do sound heartless and unfeeling."

***

A day that was unpromising now worsened; a friend rang to say their car was out of action, and could Claire give her husband a lift? When she passed this news on to her husband, he gave a short but mirthless laugh.

"Well, into each life some rain....."

"Shut up."

Gerry Ferguson was a good man---a good neighbour and a good provider for his family---but really, was that enough? His wife and daughters seemed to be fond of him, but she found him very, very hard going; he was one of life's flatteners, the sort of person who would pick apart a joke after it had been told, and who would recount even the most ordinary events in his day at great length, seeming to believe that others would find every detail riveting.

How many times had she interrupted one of his monologues---with a smile---"and to cut to the chase, Gerry......." only to have him go on as if she hadn't spoken? Don had contributed once, with annoying serenity, "well honey, some people are just like that", but it hadn't escaped her that he avoided the man at parties and barbecues.

This morning she would attack first, bringing up newsy subjects and demanding snappy opinions---frequently moving the goal posts---but the plan worked for barely a kilometre; before they had even reached the main road he had launched into the details of 'an absolutely fascinating article' he had read in an electronics magazine the night before. In desperation she considered turning up the radio---"oh I love this song, don't you?"---but that had seemed just too rude. She took refuge in a kind of coma for the rest of the journey.

Although she was well prepared for the tutorial, she reviewed her notes in her office again. Was there something more she could inject into this session on the Balkans---more intrigues, more power struggles, more assassinations? For God's sake, weren't there enough! What did they *want*? What would it take to grab the interest of this group---even of just one or two of them?

The course she had designed had been praised in other quarters, even by lecturers at other universities. And, while she thought about it, *particularly* at other universities. That was something else she had complained to Don about---the lack of generosity amongst her colleagues. And *colleagues*---that was a laugh. The department was riddled with jealousy, the members, it seemed to her, consumed with back-biting; if they read each other's lecture notes or papers at all, was it only to identify errors?

Don had suggested again that she leave the place. "Do private tutoring, at home here if you like: I'm earning enough for us to live on. It's not worth the grief darling." But no, damn them, she would keep going---and surely she would be rewarded now and then with a gifted or motivated student?

***

She was possibly halfway through the two hour session when she realised what the boy was doing. He was seated on the end of the second row, but more or less obscured from her view by the tall and bulkier student in front of him; it had registered with her that he was looking down quite a lot. She had thought---had hoped---that he was making notes, but the short and rapid vertical movement of what she could see of his shoulder eventually told her it was something different. She felt a rush of anger; hadn't she made clear more than once that there was to be no use of mobile phones during her tutorials, and no texting? She knew that the young ones practically lived on the things, but she wasn't having that here.

She often walked about during her tutorials, and now, as she began to do this, she saw him make a quick downward movement with his arm; good, he knows I'm onto him; I'll speak to him when we're finished. As she was passing the offender however, her foot came down on something; she was unable to prevent herself from putting the full weight of her heel on it, and she felt and heard the crack.

"Oh---I didn't see your mobile phone there."

"It's my new I-phone." There was real dismay in the lad's voice. "Dad gave it to me. It's busted."

She extended her hand and he put the object into it. "Perhaps it's only the glass that's cracked. I think they should be able to replace that."

"No." He looked about to burst into tears. "You don't understand. It's---it's....."

She said she was sorry, and did feel genuine compassion for the boy; he would probably have a hard time explaining to his father how the expensive gift had come to be smashed.

***

She continued across behind the students, intending now to walk up the other aisle to the front of the room, but the morning's mobile phone dramas were not over. She had just passed the back row when she heard a quiet "professor?"

As she turned to face the speaker, a somewhat shy older woman who rarely said anything, she lost her balance a little, and in an effort to regain it, put one foot behind her. The sound that followed was sickeningly familiar. This time it was Adam who cried out; he swooped down and picked up the phone. She could see that her heel had not merely fractured the front but had virtually pulverised the thing.

She was genuinely at a loss as to why she hadn't noticed it, as she had been looking down as she walked. Perhaps the young man had knocked it with his foot just as she turned; he was staring at it now.

"I'm terribly sorry Adam. What was it doing....?" She didn't finish the sentence; it could have sounded unfeeling. "I didn't see it" But what *was* it doing there; had he put it down because he had been texting too?

At the front again she made a short speech about being sorry for smashing the phones, but that she thought they had reached an understanding about mobile phones and so she had not taken into account that there could be any on the carpet. It was a logical excuse, but she knew it would not count for much with the two traumatised individuals---and she wondered if the rest were thinking she had done it deliberately.

Would the incident get around the uni---perhaps even reach the staff room? "That's Claire Harmer---you know, the one who smashed those mobile phones. Got away with it too."

At the end of the tutorial Adam came up to her and said he realised it had just been an accident. It was a moment of grace, and partly in response to that and partly because he looked not unlike their Michael, she had to stifle an urge to stand and give him a hug.

***

As she gathered up her papers and walked to the door, she hummed to herself; her mood had lightened. In the corridor she passed two older lecturers from the faculty, men who usually gave her no more than a nod of recognition; this time she forced a more enthusiastic greeting from them with a ringing 'hello' and a wide smile.

You would do well to be more pleasant to me, for I am the Wicked Witch of the History Department.

***

There was a message on her phone from the Vice-Chancellor's office reminding her about his evening party; this would be only her second since making Associate.

She had looked forward to the first one, a chance to meet informally with high-profile and even famous older academics from different faculties---a chance to 'network'---but she had been disappointed. First she had seen that the 'big names' were corralled off into a semi-separate group, from which the likes of junior professors were kept at bay by the VC's minders. She had had to make do with lesser lights, and at first she thought that could still be interesting and enjoyable, but what she found was the almost universal tendency of the men---and they were nearly all men---to talk exclusively about themselves and their own work, displaying no interest at all in her. If they did talk about 'colleagues', it was invariably in a derogatory way. She had found it hard to shift them onto different subjects. The whole evening had been tedious; she'd extracted a promise from Don to accompany her to this one.

Before the VC's thing though would be this 'rally' of the Dean, a three-monthly affair that was, if anything, even more of a time-waster. The espoused aim of the man was 'to foster a conversation about how our Faculty is working.' In his circular to staff he had posed questions: 'are we achieving what we want; do you have any suggestions for improving our results; is there enough cross-departmental communication; do you feel you are being adequately supported by the administration staff; am *I* doing enough to help?'

She supposed it may have proved worthwhile---*could* have achieved something---but not the way Carmichael operated it. While he promoted the thing as 'democracy in action,' he actually controlled the agenda. It was obvious to her that he had organised most of the submissions, and then he personally expanded on each at length. He gave short shrift to any new suggestions that came up during the actual event, promising only to 'take them on board'.

All of this fitted with what she had come to realise about the man. He was ambitious, something with which, in itself, she had no issue, but unfortunately he had no real interest in any of the members of the faculty, unless he saw in them a way of achieving some advancement for himself. He would scarcely acknowledge most members of the faculty when he passed them on campus, but let there be a favourable review of one of their papers, or the Vice-Chancellor happen to have said that he had heard 'good reports' of someone, and he would be 'best friends'.

Don had counselled her. "These strong views you take about people hurt you babe. People are imperfect. I'm imperfect. You, dare I say it, are imperfect; be cool---roll with things." She knew he was right, to a point, and she believed she *was* tolerant---by and large---but there were some people......

***

She had decided she would have lunch at the Canteen; she had heard that the food there had improved lately; 'Mediterranean' had been mentioned. She was about to leave her office when the phone rang---the Dean's secretary; could she give a brief address at the rally after lunch on how she got the best from her tutorials. When, puzzled, she asked the woman if she knew why her boss was asking her, she was told that the Dean had instructed her to say she was to take it as a compliment---that he had heard that she was very effective in that area, and that what she had to pass on would surely be of help to the newer staff.

As she walked to the canteen, she thought she might cut her lunch break short to do some preparation for the talk, but decided that this was one time she could probably just wing it. In any case, the man, if he ran true to form, would be continually interrupting her, "clarifying" things, and " respectfully" suggesting little improvements to her methods---all with that damn false smile. I am just a humble Dean interpolating some possibly useful elements. An unpleasant man. Sorry Don.

***

She managed to find an unoccupied table, but within a few minutes she was joined by the last two people she would have chosen---the Dean and his secretary.

That woman---girl really---was someone she had found pleasant enough, on the few occasions she had talked with her while in the Dean's office, but the reason she did not want to spend any time in her company now---in *their* company---was that she knew there was a relationship between the couple.

The man's attentions to the girl were obvious to everyone. And the silly girl was lapping them up. Did she not know anything about the man's past, his reputation for bedding any attractive young woman who had the misfortune to come into his orbit? If the man was not actually sleeping with this one, she believed it was only because he knew it could be professional suicide; it was widely known that he was angling for the Vice-Chancellorship of a big southern university, and knowledge of any 'improper' relationship could kill any chance there.

"Ah Claire. Looking forward to your little talk this afternoon. Hope you don't mind my asking you at such short notice? You know Alyssa don't you?" The girl and she exchanged nods and smiles.

He hoped she didn't mind their joining her at her table. She shook her head and smiled---see, I can do this Don---but what *she* hoped was that the man would be content to confine himself to inconsequential chat, or, preferably, not talk at all. But this was not to be; the man thought he'd 'run a new idea' past her---to do with the inducting of new students next year into the faculty: a plan to have staff prepare short summaries of their courses---"lively ones, let the students see that we are real people here."

She murmured something positive but the man continued in full flight, about the tremendous benefits this could bring, and how this would put the faculty on the cutting edge of fostering better student/staff relations. Ah yes, she thought, and put another tick beside your name, to help you up the academic ladder. Someone on some Senate might be moved to say, "Carmichael introduced that protocol on staff/student interaction. Good move that. We need someone with that kind of initiative for.....", whatever job they were looking to fill. The Vice-Chancellorship of that uni in Victoria perhaps; she hoped he got it.

She took refuge in femininity, deciding to admire the girl's bracelet of silver with opal inlays. "That's beautiful Alyssa."

"Thank you. I love it."

"Is it new?"

"Yes," and she held out her arm and turned it so that the different planes in the opals caught the light. "It was a gift," she said, and looked at the Dean as she said this.

Ah---this flirtation was beginning to cost. She wondered if Amanda had noticed any new large deductions from their joint bank account, if they had one. She lifted her gaze from the bauble---and saw the woman herself approaching. She felt a spasm of apprehension, but then excitement; lunch was about to become interesting.

She was looking at the Dean's face as his wife called and there was a momentary look of alarm; he swivelled around in his chair to face her. "Sweetheart," he said, and she had to admit, with every indication of pleasure. "You know the VC's do is not till six?"

"Yes, but I've two tutorials to attend. Hello Claire. I'm doing a part-time Sociology thing with Donaldson. Loving it."

The Dean had stood. "Will you have some lunch with us?"

"Yes. I'm starving. Whatever you're having."

"You know Alyssa of course."

"Yes. How are you Alyssa?"

She thought the girl looked uncomfortable. Well, welcome to the grown-up's world dear. The Dean himself looked edgy; he stood and re-arranged chairs and then offered to go back to the servery counter to place an extra order; he would bring everyone's food on a tray.

She tried to fill what she now personally found to be an awkward moment by asking for Amanda's latest news, and about her children, two of whom she knew were away at a university in the capital.

"You would already have done Sociology?"

"I did, but you know how things change. New trends. I thought this was a way of catching up, in case I decide to work again."

"Are you thinking of that?"

"Yes. With both of the boys gone, and Samantha finishing Year 12 soon; she wants to travel with a couple of friends in her gap year, so I'll have no-one depending on me."

"Except Geoffrey."

The woman gave her a look, which she couldn't read. Over Amanda's shoulder she could see the man back at the counter placing dishes of food onto a tray. This is a buzz, she thought---like something from a French movie where members of a love triangle share a scene in a civilised manner. She decided to throw a bomb into the scene.

"Alyssa was just showing me her new bracelet." The girl extended her arm; the bracelet suddenly looked more expensive.

"It's a gift. The sly minx isn't saying from whom."

"Someone special I would say," said Amanda.

"That's what I thought. And I don't mean to seem crass, but someone who has a good income."

The girl withdrew her arm.

"What are you discussing?" The man was back, putting dishes onto the table.

"Oh, it's just girl talk. I asked Alyssa to show your wife her new bracelet."

She glanced at Amanda, to observe that the woman was now looking straight ahead, and in an unfocused way. Have I just caused something to happen, she wondered, a penny to drop? The woman turned her head and looked directly at her and she thought, yes.

***

She was talking with one of the others in the staff room when the Dean arrived at two. She did not see him walk in but felt the stir around her that signalled it. The man did a quick tour of the room, greeting and being greeted. When he came to her he said "Claire--- ready to give your little speech?"

"Yes. I thought I'd run through how I prepare for a tutorial, with an emphasis....." but he was not listening. He interrupted her.

"Good. Excellent. By the way, Amanda told me after our lunch how much she enjoyed meeting up with you."

"That's nice Geoffrey. I like your wife. I would like to spend more time with her but we both seem to be so busy."

"Yes---modern women. What a long way we've come in that respect. Germaine Greer has a lot to answer for."

"Yes---like equality."

"Yes---but not I think in every respect."

"No?"

"Jewellery. Women still covet jewels," and with that he kept his eyes on her, unsmilingly.

162

"Well that's true---some more than most. Actually I have a theory that it's men who value jewellery more, in a different way. Many see the giving of jewellery as a way of declaring ownership of women. Whether they are married to them or not." Straight back, between the eyes. The man said 'interesting' and smiled and nodded to the others in the group and walked off; she thought, I have probably just killed off any chance of a full professorship while he is Dean.

***

She gave her talk, with blessedly few interruptions, and then the man himself gave his. As it seemed he was approaching the end of it, and that no new 'initiative' was being foisted onto them, he surprised her. It had come to his attention, he said, that some faculty members were having difficulties in lectures and tutorials, in the area of discipline.

"I am remiss in that I did not realise this sooner but, better late than never, I have decided to act. I am going to commission a monthly audit of this issue, where each of you will give an account of any problem that you might be having, and of course any action you have taken that has been successful in overcoming it. Compiling this audit will be the job of Claire Harmer, who I feel probably has her own effective ways of overcoming problems in tutorials; I am sure many of you will already be aware of her unique method of handling the misuse of mobile phones." A smile from him, and, she noticed, many more smiles around the room.

"You'd have no trouble doing that Claire?" looking across at her. She smiled and shook her head, but knew that she was being punished. More workload---and work that was going to make her downright unpopular with a lot of people.

Carmichael came up to her shortly afterwards. "I took the trouble of looking at your schedule Claire, and you have one of the lightest in the faculty, so I thought you were best placed to do this."

"I negotiated that lighter schedule Geoffrey, on lower pay as you know; I am part-time at the moment, and want to remain that way."

"And so you will. Unless you decide some time that you wish to leave, which would of course be up to you---though we would all be very sad to see you go." Yes, she thought, battle has been joined.

***

She was surprised to find her husband's car still in their driveway.

"After you left I felt worse."

"I'd better go and get you something from the chemist."

"No it's okay. We have plenty of stuff in the cupboard. I've taken Paracetamol and lots of water."

"Have you had anything to eat?"

"Didn't want anything."

"Do you think I should take you to a doctor?"

"No, it's a cold I'm pretty sure. Or one of those twenty-four hour things. I'm actually feeling a bit better now---better than I did at midday I can tell you. But I don't think I can come with you tonight."

She continued standing in the bedroom doorway looking at her husband. He was on his side, with the blanket pulled right up; all she could see of him was the back of his head---but I love the back of that head she thought. She shook off her shoes, slipped out of her dress, pulled aside the blanket and snuggled into his back.

"Darling, I'm infectious," alarm in his voice.

"Just don't breathe on me. I'll stay safe," and she kissed the back of his neck. His free arm came over her body and his hand cupped her bottom. "I love your gluteus maximus" he said, "both of them," as he caressed her through her slip. She snuggled into his warmth.

She felt almost giddy with happiness. I've got this, she thought, or thought she only thought, because he said "what?"

***

When it was time to dress she decided to glam up---black jersey, new drop earrings, crimson lipstick and red high heels. She demanded that her husband turn over and look at her.

"Wow! Honey, you look fabulous."

She vamped to the door, humming "Big Spender".

***

She had crossed the foyer and was about to enter the hall when she turned back and left her bag in the car; she would fly free tonight.

The room was still only half full, and neither the Dean nor the VC had yet arrived. She accepted a glass from one of the young waiters and began to mingle.

At twenty past seven the "official' party arrived, the VC and the Deans of all the faculties, her own Dean at the VC's elbow, his wife a few paces behind. She noticed that the woman was still wearing the same dress as earlier but had done something with her hair, and added a softly looped shawl, pinned with a brooch. You know what suits you, she thought.

***

Whether it was the two flutes of bubbly or what she didn't know, but she found she was enjoying the evening. She had never been a shy person, so going up to people to whom she had only ever been introduced---even to ones she had never met---was not a drama. The VC, flatteringly, remembered her name.

There were sofas here and there and after an hour and a half she decided to use one. She thought if she sat at one end, people might occasionally join her, and this happened. A man would appear, stay for a while chatting, another would appear and the first would move on; she felt like a guest of honour.

Several of her visitors brought up her breaking of the students' mobile phones, and she realised that the news must have gone right round the uni. Those who mentioned it thought it was a good thing ---a strike for discipline; they seemed almost delighted. Though she protested that they had been accidents, she could tell that they preferred to believe otherwise.

Amanda appeared, and asked if she might join her. "I've noticed that while you have been sitting here you've had a stream of courtiers."

She laughed. "I know; I feel like the Queen."

"More like bees to the honey pot. You are looking pretty spiffy."

"Thank you, and I return the compliment."

"Well---some of us have to brighten up these affairs. You must have noticed how ill-groomed most male academics are?"

"With one notable exception."

"With one, as you say, notable exception. Geoffrey has always tried to dress the part, right from when I first met him."

"Which was when?"

"At uni. I was in the first year of my Arts course and he was a lecturer."

"A cradle snatcher," but said with a smile.

"Still is."

She felt a touch awkward at that, and thought it would be a good idea to change the subject. "Have you heard about my rampage with the mobile phones?"

"Yes."

"God, I won't be able to go anywhere without---Amanda, they were accidents."

"Both of them?"

"See, even you...." She sighed. "It's hopeless. Amanda, the second boy must have knocked it out with his shoe; you know how slippery they are." She was silent for a moment, and then, despite herself, she giggled.

"Well if I were you I wouldn't say any more about it. Let people think you are a powerful woman who won't stand for any nonsense. It won't do you any harm. Quite the opposite I would think."

"It could be the main reason people have been coming up to me tonight. Or were. They've stopped now you're here."

"Would you like me to move on?"

"No, please don't. It's been all men so far."

A space in the gathering opened and they had a clear view of the woman's husband. It seemed inevitable that he should be their next topic.

"I've heard about Geoffrey's plan that you survey the others about discipline. You realise this is a punishment? For the bracelet thing?"

"I do."

"What do you think?"

She wondered for a moment if the woman was referring to the bracelet and what it signified, but then Amanda continued. "About these reports?"

She shrugged. "I think---they'll come to nothing."

"Really?"

"Well, can you imagine these men talking about any difficulties they are having in their tutorials? To a woman? And in particular, to me? They won't admit to any."

"So your reports....?"

"I'd say there'll be a couple, with nothing in them, and then your husband will think of some reason to suspend them."

They were silent for a few seconds. "You see him very clearly, don't you? You must have done psychology?"

She laughed. "Yes—didn't you?"

The other nodded. "Quite a lot."

"In any case, we are both mothers Amanda. Of boys. And that boy...." She stopped herself, then went on. "Amanda---I don't know you well and I think I would like to. But it's only right to tell you...."

The other woman cut her off. "That you don't like my husband? Or respect him? Well the news is, neither do I any more. But perhaps you shouldn't respect me either. See this?" She touched the brooch that pinned the shawl to her dress.

"Yes. I love emeralds."

"And it's a real one."

"Mmm---and are they....?"

"Diamonds. His nibs bought it for me after I found out about one of his 'friendships' two years ago. And I accepted. Whoever it was said all women are whores knew a thing or two.

Men are worse though---but they don't know it. Look at him now. He'd pimp me to the VC for a recommendation to that Victorian job." They both laughed. There was a short silence, and then "I'm leaving him."

She turned; she could see that the woman was serious.

"I haven't told him yet."

She couldn't think how to respond. She finally said "your children.....?"

"Huh. My daughter---seventeen going on thirty---has been telling me to do it for years. And the boys won't even notice. They're both boarding at that uni on the coast you know. I'll still be their mother and he will still be their father---not that he has been much of a one these last few years. So full of himself. I've given up Claire."

The memory of Don back in their bed returned to her; how nice it had been to snuggle into his warm back. "No residual love there at all, Amanda?"

"Honestly, no. And don't feel sad for me. Since I made my decision I have felt---free." She reached for Amanda's hand and clasped it. She wondered what they looked like to the rest of the gathering. Secret women's business here.

***

She rang her husband before she left the party. He was up and feeling quite a lot better he said; he had had a hot bath.

On the drive home she thought that Don would probably have aired the bed, and put clean sheets and pillow slips on; he could have tidied up the kitchen from the morning. He might have put a bottle of bubbly in the fridge---might even be getting the ingredients together for one of his little savoury omelettes.

And when he asked how her day had been, she would say that, really, it had been the best.

SIXTEEN

THIS MAN AND THIS WOMAN

It was a sunny day and she suggested they eat outside in the courtyard of the café. They settled at a table half-shaded by an ornamental grapevine and ordered their food. They made small talk for a while about mutual acquaintances, when, with no lead up at all, she proposed that they live together.

Before he could say anything the waiter arrived with the food, and his companion did little things with the cutlery and the condiments. As if by mutual agreement there was no more said on the subject while they ate, but his mind was in turmoil; she had spoken the words he had for years so longed to hear.

***

He had lived on his own for the past fifteen years, since his divorce. The end of that marriage had actually come two years before that, when his wife had told him she would be leaving; the details of that morning were still vivid in his memory.

Their youngest had just gone out the door, on her way to high school, and they were having their final cup of tea and slice of toast before going down into the town to open up their business, the timber and hardware store they had begun together while they were still in their twenties. He had just said he would have to check first thing on a consignment of flooring that was overdue when she made her announcement.

***

He had of course recognised they were drifting apart---or, really, that she was drifting away from him; she no longer shared her interests with him, and her social life did not include him. He had admitted to himself that she probably no longer loved him, but still he had hoped that they might be able to continue living together--- sharing the business---sharing the house---sharing the parenting of their three girls---sharing grandparenting eventually.

She had driven off to the store in her car, but he had not followed; he had gone back into their lounge room and sat in his chair---the one he occupied every night while they were watching television. They had been married for twenty years---had known each other since they were teenagers; so much was about to be swept away. He cried.

***

They hadn't talked about it that day at the store, and thankfully they were both kept very busy, but that evening she told him how things would be. They would share the house until Emily had left, but would have separate bedrooms; she would no longer work in their business---she would work for a friend, in real estate.

Not only did they begin to use separate bedrooms but at her instigation they created separate living quarters within the house, even with separate driveways and entrances. Whenever either of their older girls came home they still managed to do 'the family thing', and when old friends visited, they entertained them as a couple. He cherished those occasions---and took pleasure the rest of the time in simply knowing that she was nearby.

Emma left to start her university course and within a week his wife was gone.

***

She had told him she wanted to buy her own house, and to get the money for that they would have to sell the old place---the house in which he had grown up; he had found that very hard. Then she had demanded they sell the business. He had resisted that, proposing that he give her so much each year until a final agreed sum was reached, but she had insisted on the full lump sum up front; she wanted to set up her own gift shop.

Instead of selling, he borrowed from the bank and paid her out. Some of his friends said he was being very generous, but he defended her, saying that it was only fair, she did rightly own half of the business.

***

He had found it tough going for the first few years, barely able to meet the loan repayments. It was only when a new mine opened in the district and construction began on many new houses that he began to get ahead. He expanded the building and added many new lines; profits increased.

He bought an investment apartment; he was elected President of the Chamber of Commerce; he took a holiday in Europe. A big national company offered to buy him out, but he turned them down; the business continued to expand.

***

Her crafts and gifts gallery always looked busy to him, though she never revealed, whenever they met, exactly how well she was doing. Then he learned---from others---that she had leased a bigger building and brought in a partner, a female friend from her school days. That friend he heard had ambitions to expand, to have a

173

number of different shops in the one building. He knew the woman reasonably well---and her husband slightly---and he guessed that the bigger ambition was coming as much from him as from her.

He had never had much time for the woman, who he had always thought was somewhat superficial and opportunistic, and he certainly had no time for the husband. He did not trust a man who was always talking about 'deals', and forever speculating on the wealth of some of his acquaintances, as though he were lining them up for propositions. He certainly would not have chosen to have anything to do with him when it came to business.

He wondered whether he should reveal his doubts to her, and eventually he did, but she told him to keep his opinions to himself, and that in any case she was in partnership with her friend, not the husband. Their expansion went ahead.

***

She too became a member of the Chamber. She took an active part at each meeting, and he thought she spoke well on any issue that arose; he saw that the other members respected her. He was genuinely glad for her---pleased with the mark she was making.

***

Then, some years later, at a party to which both of them had been invited, she told him she had plans to expand again---to buy the shops on either side. The partners intended to knock down the walls between and turn the whole space into a large court, inviting other shop owners to set up within it; they wanted to have furniture and modern kitchen things, and a restaurant serving full lunches. Her friend's husband was now a partner too, and he had persuaded them that the town was ready for a place like that.

He had heard some more worrying things about the husband, and told her of them, but once again she waved them away.

He occasionally escorted other women to parties or race meetings or other functions, but no romance ever developed. She did not take another partner either. He did not know why that was---for her---but for himself, he knew that he had never really moved on. He might think he had, but then a chance meeting, even just glimpse of her across the street, told him that he hadn't.

The continuing single status of both of them encouraged their three girls in a campaign to bring them together again. "Mum still doesn't have anyone Dad. And you don't. And you know you still have a crush on her."

He wasn't annoyed by their efforts, but he couldn't think how to reply when they said these things; he would just smile and shake his head. They didn't understand that it would only happen if *she* wanted it; she had always called that tune.

***

He had been twenty and she nineteen when they had started going out together. Before this, at High School and for a year or two afterwards, he had scarcely ever spoken to her, but then she had always had a boyfriend in tow, and behind that one a conga line of would-be's. Eventually though he had plucked up the courage to ask her to a dance---the first time he had ever asked a girl out---and she had agreed.

***

He let her know he would always be available if she were ever short of an escort to a party or a dance, and in time they did go out together more and more, until eventually he was her 'steady'.

He had wondered sometimes, in their later life, if she had agreed to marry him chiefly because he had always *been* there---'Mister Reliable'. Her parents liked him---or at least approved of him; had her mother or her father told her he would be a wise choice? "He'll look after you."

He *had* looked after her too, and the girls when they came along---'a good provider', people said. He had prided himself on that, but he knew---he knew---he was not 'exciting', was in fact probably considered by her friends to be a bit dull, and after twenty years of being in harness with this willing but plodding horse, his wife had decided to cut the traces.

***

She invited him to the opening of their court. It was a big deal---a very big deal---with not only the mayor and most of the council present but also the local member of parliament, as well as most of their town's 'society'. The place was festooned with lights and bunting---even the street outside---and there was a band, and lavish catering. It was the biggest party the town had seen since the council had put on the show for Charles and Diana's wedding.

She looked terrific that night---glamorous and confident. He found himself frequently looking at her---from a distance---and, he thought, discreetly. All three of their daughters had come back for their mother's big night. "Doesn't she look great, Dad?"

***

It was only a few months afterwards though that he began to hear rumours---that the trio had been able to lease out only a few of the shops, and bills were not being paid. He wondered if he should offer to help in some way; his business---their old one---was booming. He sent her a note, wishing her well and hinting at assistance, but he received no reply.

***

Within a year the whole venture had collapsed, not only into receivership but with talk of fraud. He couldn't believe that his wife was involved in anything like that, though he was prepared to believe it of her friend, and certainly of the friend's husband. The man in fact disappeared, and a warrant was issued for his arrest.

He learned that she had had to sell her house, and was now renting. He left a message on her phone, inviting her to borrow some of his funds if she needed them---money he would in fact have gladly *given* her; he received no reply once again.

***

The big national company returned with such a huge offer for his business he realised he would be foolish to reject it; when he visited his solicitor's office to sign the paperwork he saw that she was working there as a secretary.

***

Their eldest rang, just to say hello she said, but then asked if he had seen her mother lately. Did they ever have lunch together? Why didn't they? Then the woman herself rang just a day later---he wondered if the two had talked. She asked to meet him for lunch, at the nice little cafe near her office, and after they had ordered the food she had, with the poise that was so typical of her, put her proposition.

***

They finished eating and the waiter took their plates away. She looked at him expectantly; he had to respond---but what to say? He took a breath---and her mobile phone rang; there was a client in the office she said, and they couldn't find his file; she had to go straight back. She kissed him on the cheek.

***

He looked around at the other tables and the dozen or so people sitting there. Had any of them taken notice of his companion? He was sure some would have, she was still a striking looking woman. He wondered what they saw when they looked at him: a fairly nondescript older citizen? An oddly matched couple surely.

For some reason the phrase 'this man and this woman' came into his mind; weren't they words from the marriage ceremony? And now he had just heard other words, words that he had so long yearned to hear, yet he had not immediately said yes. Why was that?

***

His mind had been in a whirl all through the meal, but now it was beginning to settle. He leant back in his seat; there was a patch of sun near him and he stretched his legs out into it. It was really very pleasant there; he could stay a while longer---perhaps have another glass of wine. He did have things to do and decisions to make, about the winding up of his business, but they could wait--- everything could wait; it was always better to think things through. There was no urgency---no urgency about anything really.

SEVENTEEN

THE TRIAL OF PETER HALVORSEN

"Have you visited our cemetery yet?" This from our Town Librarian.

"The cemetery? No, should I?"

"Well---you have a strong curiosity about our town---and its citizens." Diplomatically said, but she had me pegged, after my few months of residence in her town; others might have said 'nosy'.

"Any headstones in particular I should look at?"

She nodded. "Second row from the back. Barry Patterson."

***

"BARRY EDWARD PATTERSON 1940 - 1964 TAKEN SUDDENLY." I was reading to Jessica from the note I had made at the cemetery.

"Anything else?"

"Yes. Across TAKEN SUDDENLY---someone had written 'MURDERED' in chalk. Did you know that was there?"

"No, but there's always something. It'll be the Patterson family, or one of their gang."

"So---murdered by whom?"

"Well, according to those people---him," and she indicated a man of about my own age sitting and reading at a table in 'Non-Fiction'. I tried not to stare.

Jessica had been holding a folder, and now she placed it on the table in front of me. On the cover was written "The Trial Of Peter Andreas Halvorsen."

"I ordered a copy of the transcript as soon as I learned about the case---not long after I took up this job. I fear I share your propensities."

"And that's Halvorsen?"

"Mmm. He comes in as often as you do. One of my best 'customers'. He'd be interesting for you to get to know."

She went off to attend to someone at the front desk; I chanced another look at the murderer and then opened the folder.

**

The Crown alleged that on Saturday 15th February 1964 Peter Halvorsen took a rifle from his home, drove to the home of Barry Patterson and there murdered the man.

**

"My name is Alan Freeman. I'm twenty four years old."

"Mister Freeman, tell us in your own words what you saw on the fifteenth of February 1964."

"That bloke shot Barry."

"The Crown notes that the witness has pointed at the Accused. It also takes the opportunity to point out to the court that Defence agrees that Mister Patterson died as a result of receiving a bullet from a rifle held by the Accused at the time.

But now Mister Freeman, I ask you to please tell us everything involving yourself that led up to the incident on that Saturday---and in order please."

"We were having a drink at the Royal after work---Barry and me. We only worked half a day on Saturdays. At Cassidy's."

"Cassidy's is...?"

"....a timber yard."

"And the "Royal"....?"

"The big pub in the main street."

"You and Mister Patterson were friends?"

"Yeah. We went to school together."

"The local high school?"

"Yeah."

"The same school that the Accused attended?"

"Yes. He was in the same year---but we weren't friends with him."

"But now, on this afternoon in the hotel bar, what were you talking about ?"

"Halvorsen---well more his dog. A dingo."

"Mister Halvorsen kept a dingo?"

"Yeah. We never liked that. They're all killers. No-one should keep one. It's wrong."

"What did you decide to do, this day, in that bar?"

"Well, it was Barry's idea. He was the one who really hated it. He was always going on about it. He reckoned we should go and get it."

"Get it?"

"Go up to Halvorsen's place. We knew he was playing cricket and wouldn't be back till later. We thought we could shove it into a cage Barry had on the back of his ute."

"And is that what you did?"

"Yeah. It wasn't easy 'cause it went feral."

"By that you mean.....?"

"Mad. It was snapping at us through the wire netting round its kennel. Barry had a noose on the end of a stick. When we got it into the crate on the ute I thought it would just about wreck it. Dingoes are wild animals you know."

"Now Mister Freeman, tell us what happened next."

"We drove in the two utes, Barry's and mine, to Barry's place. He and his missus had a house on the other side of town, on a couple of acres. It took about fifteen minutes ."

"What happened when you reached Mister Patterson's home?"

"Barry went inside to tell his missus to stay in the house---he was going to shoot the dog see---but when he came out we saw Halvorsen's ute coming down the road. The cricket match must have finished a bit early and he'd figured out we had the dog."

"Then what happened?"

"Halvorsen gets out of the ute and he's carrying a gun: a twenty-two. He marches over towards us. I didn't like the look of it, but Barry---he was a gutsy sort of a bloke---tough, you know---he walks toward him. That's when he shot him."

"Mister Halvorsen shot Mister Patterson?"

"Yes."

"And what happened next?"

"I ran inside to call the ambulance. I thought it wasn't much use though because Barry looked dead to me. Straight off."

***

I stopped reading at this point and glanced over at Halvorsen; this man looked like any other senior citizen quietly enjoying the facilities at the town's Library, but once he had been 'the Accused'.

Jessica must have been keeping an eye on me because she walked over.

"I've read only the prosecution witness bit so far. It looks bad. You could understand Halvorsen being very angry, but if you load a rifle and then come at someone......"

"Read on."

I noticed Halvorsen stacking up the books on his table; it looked as if he were about to leave.

"Jessica---Halvorsen's leaving. I want to meet him. Can you introduce us please."

"You're not going to talk about the trial?" Sternly.

"No---no I won't." I tried to think. "I want to know about dingoes. I've always been interested in them," I said.

"He still has a couple."

"Well then....."

***

My hand was taken in a strong grip. Halvorsen was of medium height, broad shouldered and fit looking; he looked as if he could still give a good account of himself on the cricket field. He had a full head of hair, greying, but showing still some blond; adding to the blue eyes---and of course the name---one could easily think Scandinavian.

Jessica had brought him to my table; I had turned her folder upside down. I began asking some questions about our native dog, but I only half listened to his answers, my mind and my senses more or less consumed by what I had just read; sitting opposite me was someone who had taken a loaded rifle to another man's house and had subsequently been charged with *murder*.

However I must have shown sufficient interest in what he was saying about the animals for Halvorsen to invite me to his place to see his dingoes for myself. We arranged it for mid-morning the next day.

After he had departed I went back to the folder but decided it would be more interesting to have this meeting with him before I read any further. I handed the folder back to Jessica and told her of the planned visit.

"Are you really interested in dingoes?" She gave me what I would describe as 'a searching look'; was this merely a morbid interest in a person once tried for murder?

"Well I am. I've always been rather attracted to the look of the animal---and I'll see them close up tomorrow for the first time, and be talking to someone who really knows a lot about them. But---yes---the man interests me too. I'll try not to bring up the trial. Promise."

***

He met me at the front door of his house---the house he told me he had lived in since birth---and took me down a hallway into the kitchen and made us a pot of tea. I noticed "The Australian" newspaper of the previous day open on the kitchen table; when I raised an issue that had been dealt with at length in the Commentary section of that issue I found he was across it, and had a view about it. I was beginning to think that this might be an interesting person for a newcomer to the town to get to know.

He took me out into a back garden of neat vegetable beds and healthy looking fruit trees. There were aviaries of finches and budgerigars and parrots, and a loft of homing pigeons; he went to the loft and opened the trapdoor to give them a fly. "I lose the odd one. Hawks."

At the rear of the garden was a fowl run---"can you use some eggs?"---and two kennels with wire enclosed runs. There was a dingo in each---typical in appearance of that golden haired breed. He greeted one and let him out. The dog walked straight over to me and smelled my leg.

" Don't try to pat Rex; he doesn't like that. Just offer him the back of your hand."

I did this; the animal sniffed it and then trotted away, beginning a slow circuit of the garden, just inside the wire fence. "He's checking if there's been any intruder into his territory."

"Very cool."

"Yes, that's typical. Very different to Sam," and as he said this a black Labrador came bounding towards us from behind a shed and leapt at the man. They wrestled for a minute till Halvorsen told the dog to sit.

I walked over to the other kennel and looked at the dog there; it looked identical to Rex.

"You house them separately?"

"Yes, they seem to prefer that. Solitary beasts." Three of you possibly, I thought.

***

In the mid-afternoon I called at the Library again and Jessica picked up the folder which was on her desk and handed it to me.

"I thought you'd be back today. Have an interesting visit?"

"Very. The man is stimulating company. And I have eggs, if you're interested. And apricots."

"Thanks, I'll take both. The trial didn't 'come up'?"

"I never mentioned it. But I suspect he's onto me."

***

Defence began cross-examining the witness.

"Mister Freeman, you have given evidence that you and Mister Patterson arrived at Mister Patterson's house with the dingo and that very shortly afterwards the Accused also arrived in his utility. He approached you quickly you said, Mister Patterson went towards him and Mister Halvorsen then shot Mister Patterson. Is that a correct summary of your testimony?"

"Yes."

"Was that all that happened?"

"Yes it was---more or less."

"More or less? Please tell us again---and leave out no detail."

"Well---when Barry came out of the house---before Halvorsen got there---he said we should have some fun with the dog. He wanted him to fight one of his pig dogs."

"And what are pig dogs?"

"Dogs you use to catch pigs of course. Wild pigs."

"And can you describe a typical pig dog."

"They've gotta be solid---it takes a lot to hold a pig, especially a big one---like a boar. There's Bull Terrier in a lot of them---they don't let go. But bigger breeds too---Wolfhound sometimes. They get ripped up sometimes by a pig. You usually just stitch them up. You only keep the game ones."

"Would most of these pig dogs be bigger than a dingo?"

"Heaps."

"So would it be what you might call a fair fight, between this dingo and one of Mister Patterson's pig dogs?"

"Objection Your Honour," said the Prosecutor. "The Defence is calling for an opinion on the part of the witness."

"I will allow this," said the Judge. "Mister Freeman seems to be well acquainted with the subject. I think he can be regarded on this point as an expert witness."

"Thank you your Honour. Would you call it a fair fight, Mister Freeman?"

"Probably not---but Barry thought it would be interesting to see how a wild dog would go."

"Did you agree to this fight?"

"Yeah. Barry was going to shoot the dingo, so what was the difference? I thought it would lose and get bunged up a lot---so we'd be putting it out of its misery anyhow---only....."

"Only what, Mister Freeman?"

"Well after Barry let the dingo out into a yard---he had a round yard for breaking in horses, with a high weld-mesh fence---nothing can get out of it. Anyhow he went and got one of his dogs and put it in there too. His dog wanted to fight straight away---went straight at the dingo---but the dingo---he had to protect himself see---he managed to get a grip on the other dogs neck, and he wouldn't let go. He more or less choked that dog."

"To death?"

"Yeah. Barry was wild."

"So did he decide to shoot the dingo then?"

"No, he---he went and got another one of his dogs and put it in."

"And what happened this time?"

"Barry's dog got a good grip first. One of the dingo's front legs. You could see that he broke it."

At this point the Prosecutor objected; what relevance could there be in this line of questioning to the defence of the Accused? The judge put the objection to the Defence Counsel, who replied that because the Accused knew Mister Patterson had pig dogs, and that something of this nature could well be happening there, it went a long way to explaining his subsequent actions. The judge allowed a continuation.

"This may be distressing to some members of the jury and I am sorry, but I think we need to go through it. Can you remember what happened next, Mister Freeman?"

"The bottom part of the dingo's leg broke off in the dog's mouth and the dingo was able to grab Barry's dog round the neck---like the first one. He killed that one too."

"Then what happened ?"

"Well Barry got his biggest one---we call it the Monster. I've seen it pull down tuskers. This dog went straight at the dingo and ripped him right along the side---you could see the ribs. The dingo had had it then I thought; Barry's dog sort of stood back a minute and the dingo was trying to stand on three legs and there was a lot of blood coming from his side. And that's when Halvorsen arrived and shot Barry."

"Now---you earlier testified that when the accused arrived at Mister Patterson's place he hurried toward you both with a loaded rifle and that when Mister Patterson went towards him he shot him. We now know that the dingo had first been put into a small yard from which it could not escape and had fought two pig dogs to the death and had now been badly wounded by a third. Is this in fact the moment when Mister Halvorsen arrived in his ute?"

"Well, yes."

"And when Mister Halvorsen got out of his utility, did he walk immediately towards Mister Patterson and shoot him, as you earlier testified?"

"Yes."

***

I stopped reading---as I sometimes do when I am reading a crime novel and I believe that I have reached a pivotal moment. I wondered what I would be now thinking if I had been a member of the jury at this trial. I would have been less than impressed with the witness; he had already misled us once concerning the sequence of events at Patterson's; he could be misleading us again. On the other hand, he was the only person living---besides Halvorsen---who had seen what happened that day.

I expected that the Defence would be calling Halvorsen to the stand next. Not so.

***

"I tender a post mortem report on the dingo in question, carried out by Janette Mortenson, a veterinarian of this town. In it she details not only the injuries we have heard described today but also the presence of a fresh bullet wound. Mister Freeman, can you tell us how that wound was sustained?"

Though the transcript does not indicate any pause before Freeman's reply to this question, I bet there would have been one. And if I had been in that jury, I think I would have been leaning forward, metaphorically speaking, to hear his reply.

"Halvorsen shot him."

"Mister Halvorsen shot his own animal?"

"Yes."

"So---will you please outline carefully, once again, the order of events after Mister Halvorsen pulled up in his utility."

"Well, he walked straight up to the fence of the round yard and aimed at his dog and shot him."

"What happened next?"

"Then he reloaded the .22 and shot Barry."

"Did Mister Halvorsen aim the rifle at Mister Patterson?"

" Well----yes."

"Mister Freeman, you earlier testified that you and Mister Patterson had barely arrived at Mister Patterson's property when the accused arrived in his utility. You have since told us that first Mister Patterson had forced the dingo to defend itself against attacks from three of his pig dogs before the accused arrived. You also said that the accused walked straight towards you when he got out of his utility and shot Mister Patterson, but you have since told us that instead, the accused walked straight to the yard where the animals were fighting and shot his dingo. You have also said that the accused reloaded his rifle. Now Mister Freeman, in your own time, please tell us very carefully what happened next."

"Well---Halvorsen aimed the gun at his dog again. He hadn't hit it cleanly the first time---too high. But Barry barrelled him."

"Hit him with his body?"

"Yeah---but Halvorsen was sort of leaning into the fence so he didn't go over. Then they sort of wrestled."

"While they were wrestling where was the gun?"

"Sort of between them."

"And can you remember where the barrel was pointing?"

"Up."

"And then the gun went off?"

"Yes."

"Mister Freeman, the autopsy report reveals that the bullet severed Mister Patterson's carotid artery, entering the base of his neck and travelling up through it. Would that accord with what you witnessed?"

"Yeah I reckon."

***

It seemed that out of the mouth of the prosecution's own witness the Crown's case had been demolished. The jury cannot have taken much time to reach their 'not guilty' verdict.

***

"Absolutely fascinating." I said to Jessica, who was hovering around; she could see I was on the last page.

"Justice prevailed," she said.

"Not altogether. That friend of Patterson should have copped something. He lied really; if the Defence had been a bit slack it could have gone very differently And Halvorsen lost his dog."

"True. But---and I've never talked about the trial with him---I have the strong impression that the man bears no big grudge against those families. He's 'moved on' as they say."

***

My wife and I had first visited this town many years ago, and liked it very much. As I neared retirement from teaching it had become our goal to move here. The diagnosis of cancer in my wife and then her devastatingly quick death had made me re-think the move, but after a while I had decided it would still be worth doing.

It has been good; I have been made welcome in the town, and already I have some promising friendships, such as in Jessica.

***

The man was in the Library again at the same time as myself. I went over and admitted to him that I had read the transcript. He did not seem surprised, or in any way put out.

"It was a long time ago---fifty years. But I can see you are interested. Do you have any questions?"

"Do you mind?" He shook his head.

"Well---why did you go straight to Patterson's place?"

"I was pretty sure it would be Patterson that had taken Sandy; he was the only person I'd heard of who had a real bee in his bonnet about me having a dingo."

"Why did you think that was?"

"I honestly don't know." He shrugged. "He was always antagonistic to me, even back at school---as if he couldn't stand me or something."

He paused. "If you get to know me you will find that I'm not easily stirred up, and I think in a funny way that got to Barry. I was good at schoolwork too, particularly English, and he wasn't---he had trouble learning to read and write. I think that could have got under his skin too. I don't know."

"Okay---but that day, was the rifle for protection, or......?"

"Or to shoot Patterson?" He smiled---and the smile was of such a gentle, rueful kind I was embarrassed I had allowed even a suggestion of that in my unfinished question. "No, Patterson was a roughie and a toughie but I wasn't afraid of him. I didn't hate him either or anything like that. I was just fearful of what he might have been doing to my friend. The rifle was to put an end to that---if I was right."

He paused and looked down, and I thought he was possibly remembering the scene, then he looked up at me again. "See---I'd taken that dog out of his environment. He was just a little pup when I found him; I was doing some fencing on a station up in the hills. I thought I might be able to domesticate him. And I had a young Blue Heeler at the time and I thought he might be a good companion for him; it's always better to have two dogs.

He was very smart---very observant---never lost that. He was obedient too, but always stayed a bit aloof, like you saw the other day with Rex. I was his master, but it was also like he was saying "I am your equal too". I loved that about him. And then to see him degraded in that way---I just had to put an end to it. I owed him that."

EIGHTEEN

THE TIME OF MY LIFE

When my son Bill phoned to tell me he was getting married again, he said he and Jill were intending to keep the thing pretty small and low key; it was going to be the second time round for her too. Of course I was invited, but he didn't really expect his 'old Dad' to make the long journey. (Old? Only sixty, and as fit as many men half my age!)

From my cattle station in western Queensland to Melbourne *would* be a long journey but this widower was up for it. And in fact, wild horses wouldn't have stopped me from attending, to show my eldest and his girl that I was with them on this second attempt. (And it would be an opportunity to re-acquaint myself with the city I had once known well, when I was studying agriculture at university there.)

***

I'm on quite a few committees in my district---I suppose I am considered a 'responsible' citizen---so when I drove away in my new Landcruiser, I felt a bit like a boy wagging school. Excited. Light-hearted.

Approaching Melbourne two days later, I ran into rain, and then of course much more traffic. I had been in a good mood the whole drive, but when I reached the place where the old Hume Highway gives way to Sydney Road, in the suburb of Coburg, I actually began to feel irritation, first at the number of vehicles, and then at the numbers of people. Not only were the footpaths crowded, but the roads too, people crossing with seemingly no care for their safety; I had to slow to a crawl.

They were mostly women, and wearing long coats or dresses and head scarves. I knew they were Muslim; some were even veiled.

I was unaccustomed to such things, and---it embarrasses me to admit this now---I didn't like what I was seeing.

I would have said that I accept all cultures and religions, but I wasn't in an accepting mood this day. I was visiting a city I had once known well; as a student I had actually lived quite close to Coburg, but this was not the Coburg that I remembered. I was not liking *this* Melbourne.

***

I had the sense to realise that, in my somewhat agitated state, and with the rain, there was a risk that I could hit someone. I found somewhere to park, leaned my seat back, closed my eyes and took some deep breaths.

It seemed to work, and after fifteen or so minutes I opened my eyes, shook my shoulders and eased the Landcruiser out again into the traffic; I was ready for the rest of Melbourne. I fished around in the glove box for a CD, and came up with "My Fair Lady".

 A pretty young woman with a baby in her arms was waiting at a set of lights. I smiled, and got a smile in return. Loverly.

***

Bill had booked me into a hotel on the Kingsway, quite close to the CBD. I was unpacking there when my son rang from a hotel further along that street, where he and his future in-laws were staying. "The Parkers were wondering if we could have drinks together? There's a nice lounge here on the ground floor."

"Of course, son. I'll walk down. Good idea. Who'll be there?"

"Just Mr. and Mrs. Parker and Jill's sister and her husband. Couple of others."

"Sounds harmless."

"I said I didn't know. I thought you might be tired."

"Well I'm not; I want to see you all." I really did.

"Six-thirty then?" A pause. "The Parkers will be a bit dressed up I'm afraid." Look nice Dad. I said I'd wear my dress thongs.

***

I thoroughly enjoyed the little party; I tried to make a contribution with stories of life back home on the station. Sarah, Bill's future mother-in-law, persuaded me to go shopping for gifts with her the next afternoon.

***

In the morning I was free to do whatever I liked and I decided on a walk around nearby Lake Albert. I did not get back to my hotel till after twelve.

***

"Good afternoon sir, my name is Chloe. Where would you like me to put your lunch?" A smiling, pretty girl.

"Oh, over here. Too many things on this table."

"Are you here on business sir?"

"No Chloe, I'm here for my son's wedding."

"That's nice." Hesitation. "You're on your own?"

It took me a moment. "Yes. My wife died some years ago. But this is actually my son's second marriage. He's thirty-five. I'm sixty" And then, because I thought she wouldn't take offence, "may I ask how old you are?"

"Twenty-three."

"My youngest son is twenty-six."

"And is he good looking?" There was a definitely implied 'too'.

"Yes, but no competition." She laughed and left. We had flirted.

***

I spent the afternoon shopping for wedding gifts with Sarah as planned and she dropped me back at my hotel. The rest of the wedding party had engagements that evening so I decided to once again eat in my room.

***

"Ah, Chloe."

"Good evening Mr. Watson. May I set up your table?"

"Yes---but I didn't order---smoked salmon. Or champagne. Just the 'Chef's Hamburger' and a beer."

"And that's all you'll pay for Mr. Watson. This is on me. For the wedding."

I watched as this attractive girl set my little table. I asked her how long she would be working that evening and she said ten.

"Well, would you feel like coming up here then? Have a glass with me?"

"Sure, I'd like to." As she was going out she said "see you about ten Mr. Watson."

Mister. Was I about to make a fool of myself?

"It's Hugh."

***

"Have you seen my girls lately Dad?" Bill and Jill had dropped in at my hotel, and we were having a coffee in the ground floor lounge.

"Yes---I was in Brisbane about three weeks ago. Have you met them Jill?"

"Oh yes. They were nice to me." She thought of something. "What did you get up to with my mother this afternoon? She was so happy when I saw her. She really likes you."

And I had liked her. I don't usually enjoy shopping trips but that one I had. I liked her daughter too; I thought she seemed a good match for my son.

"Did Bill ever tell you about the first girlfriend he had?"

"Dad!"

"He was eight." Bill relaxed. "Ralph had stopped being Bill's deputy in everything and Betty Garner just stepped in. Her father was our head stockman. Still works for us, as a handyman."

"She could do things I couldn't. Remember how she used to get on a horse Dad? She just climbed up its legs. Thing just stood there."

We reminisced until nine forty-five, when I excused myself. I had a date.

***

When Chloe came into the room this young woman and this 'old' man embraced immediately. Had we both expected that would happen?

Concerning what happened next, I shall merely repeat the saying that I know is a cliche but will serve here---age is only a number.

***

I woke quite late the next morning, but as the wedding wasn't until five in the afternoon I had plenty of time to spare. I thought again about my earlier rejection of the 'foreignness' of Coburg, which seemed ridiculous in retrospect. I made a decision to re-enter Coburg, and give it a second chance. Give *myself* a second chance.

***

At eleven that morning the streets and footpaths there were even more crowded and chaotic than they had been two afternoons before, but I found a park and plunged in.

***

I have fair hair and blue eyes, but it seemed everyone else had dark hair and brown eyes; when English was spoken, it was with strong accents. The crowd was divided: women shopping and moving about, and men sitting and talking together, drinking coffee on the pavements outside cafes.

The men wore suits with vests or cardigans, and no ties; many smoked, and most were not clean-shaven. To this conservative grazier type they looked 'rough'---almost dangerous. The women were dressed mainly in dark clothing, and wore what I now know are called hijabs; some of the younger ones *were* bare-headed---and didn't they have *hair*, cascades of it.

There was an open market in one big old building, with many clothing stalls, but not here the elegant calm of a David Jones; items were turned over, held up, passed to others, tried on and exclaimed over. Shopkeepers shouted to each other across the heads of their customers.

There were food stalls too, with, to my eyes, astonishing amounts and varieties of food, many of which I did not recognise. Big tins with brightly coloured labels were stacked alarmingly high. Baskets of nuts and dates and spices were everywhere. The smells were wonderful; I was in a bazaar.

I went to an open plaza to sit for a while. Three girls landed on a bench near me, as noisy as lorikeets on a branch. All had hair below their shoulders, thick and crinkled. One girl had dyed hers blonde, but fully one inch of the dark roots showed. They were talking in English about some boys across the road, killing them with ridicule. Then they flew off, to roost again near the post office, pointedly ignoring another group of boys.

I---though a senior and very 'Anglo' resident of a sparsely populated part of Queensland---felt surprisingly at home in all this exotic southern bustle and noise.

***

The wedding was at five and the reception was at the hotel where the Parkers were staying. I left after ten and walked back up to my own hotel and went to bed.

I thought I would go straight to sleep but after an hour I was still wide awake. Rather than lie there I decided to go for a drive; I went down towards St. Kilda and eventually parked beside the water. I got out and found a big boulder to sit on.

There was a light breeze coming off the Bay; I could scarcely see the water just a metre below me---well I could, but it was black. There was a strong briney smell---a good smell.

***

A vehicle drove up and strong light flooded me. I didn't get up; one of the hotel's "Do Not Disturb" signs could have been hanging on my back.

"Excuse me sir, is this your vehicle?" I turned, to see a young policeman in uniform.

"Yes it is ---constable."

"Do you have your driver's licence?"

"Yes. My wallet's in the Landcruiser." I got up; I suppose my sitting there at that time of night did look odd. "What's the problem?" I opened the door and pulled my wallet from the glove box. I heard another door on the police wagon open.

"Mr. Watson?"

"Yes?" The other policeman came into my view.

"Rick Finlayson, Mr. Watson. From 'Currie Downs'."

I put my hand up to shield my eyes against the light and recognised the young giant. The Finlaysons had had five boys in five years; when they all turned up to compete at a district gymkhana at home it always caused a lot of confusion amongst the judges.

"What are you doing all the way down here Rick?"

"I just thought I'd like to come to a different place. It's been good."

***

The boys adopted me. They said they were just about to grab a bite to eat and invited me to follow them into the main street to their favourite takeaway. We ate hamburgers on a bench beside their wagon, and I told Rick all the latest from home; his companion, Paul, was a Melbourne boy, and I tried to make the news interesting for him too. In turn I learned a lot about the life of a young policeman in Melbourne.

A call came in---a disturbance at a hotel. The young men said goodbye and drove off. I continued to sit on that bench, content to watch the passing people. Nearly all of them were young, much younger than I, but I felt young too.

I thought 'I'm having the time of my life.'

THE AUTHOR

 Ron Iddon is probably best known in Australia for his earlier work on the ABC's long running television series "A BIG COUNTRY, as a reporter and director.

He left the ABC to become an independent filmmaker, eventually writing and directing twenty more documentaries, all of which were shown on television; "Peppimenarti", about life in an Aboriginal settlement in the Northern Territory, was nominated for 'Best Documentary' in the AFI Awards.

By the mid-1980's he had three co-written non-fiction books to his credit and for the past ten years he has been writing fiction. In 2011 he released "The Short Stories of Ron Iddon – The Murray River Collection", in 2012 "The Short Stories of Ron Iddon – The Queensland Collection", and in 2013, a third collection, "The Redspear Team"

Ron lives in Toowoomba, southern Queensland. He writes every day, and also tutors in literacy. (More on his web site, *roniddon.com.au*)

EARLIER BOOKS BY THIS AUTHOR

NON-FICTION

(In collaboration)

A Big Country (John Mabey)

A Big Country (John Mabey)

The Stockman (Mary Durack, R.M.Williams et al)

FICTION

(Solo)

The Short Stories of Ron Iddon – The Murray River Collection

The Short Stories of Ron Iddon – The Queensland Collection

The Redspear Team

All collections of short stories, and this book,
are available only on the internet, via *www. roniddon.com.au*
or *www.leopardwoodproductions.com.au*

 **LEOPARDWOOD
PRODUCTIONS**